M
KNI

DATE DUE

JAN 12 2007	

DEMCO, INC. 38-2931

'Detective Inspector Jeremy Faro had not the least idea that a funeral, melancholy enough but entirely innocent of crime, would lead to a startling confession from his stepson Dr Vince Laurie and that a suicide from the unfinished Tay Bridge would open up a sinister trail of seemingly unconnected events. Events which were to culminate in one of the most baffling and personal dilemmas of his career, and a series of crimes which had tragic and far-reaching repercussions several years later . . . '

The news that Vince, resident doctor with Deane Enterprises, contractors for the Tay Bridge, is to marry Rachel Deane arouses mixed emotions in Jeremy Faro. He will miss the camaraderie of their bachelor estate, and while his stepson's happiness is his dearest wish, how can Vince possibly support an heiress? Vince's lodgings with the impoverished family of actor William McGonagall are basic indeed, while Rachel receives Faro in the sumptuous family mansion, where she completely denies any romantic attachment to Vince.

Why has she changed so suddenly from devoted fiancée to cold-hearted stranger? Are the Deanes, a byword for benevolence and fair dealing, in fact a bunch of crooks? The casualty rate amongst their employees is high and rumour has it that shoddy materials are being substituted for those originally ordered for the bridge. And how can Faro satisfactorily investigate mysterious deaths in an area outside his jurisdiction and at the same time protect his stepson from disaster?

A Quiet Death is a fascinating mesh of fact and fiction, another intriguing glimpse into the casebook of Inspector Faro in that murky sinister underworld behind the façade of Victorian respectability.

by the same author

A DRINK FOR THE BRIDGE (A novel of the Tay
  Bridge Disaster)
THE BLACK DUCHESS
CASTLE OF FOXES
COLLA'S CHILDREN
THE CLAN
ESTELLA
ENTER SECOND MURDER
BLOOD LINE
DEADLY BELOVED
KILLING COUSINS

non-fiction

THE ROBERT LOUIS STEVENSON TREASURY
STEVENSON IN THE SOUTH SEAS

A Quiet Death

An Inspector Faro Mystery

Alanna Knight

MACMILLAN
LONDON

First published 1991 by
MACMILLAN LONDON LIMITED
4 Little Essex Street London WC2R 3LF
and Basingstoke

Associated companies in Auckland, Delhi, Dublin, Gaborone,
Hamburg, Harare, Hong Kong, Johannesburg, Kuala Lumpur, Lagos,
Manzini, Melbourne, Mexico City, Nairobi, New York, Singapore
and Tokyo

ISBN 0-333-55014-5

A CIP catalogue record for this book is available from
the British Library.

Typeset by Macmillan Production Limited

Printed and bound in Great Britain by Billing and Sons Limited,
Worcester

'Better a quiet death than a public misfortune'
Old Proverb

For all my family
and many friends in Dundee

Chapter One

Detective Inspector Jeremy Faro had not the least idea that a funeral, melancholy enough but entirely innocent of crime, would lead to a startling confession from his stepson and that a suicide from the unfinished Tay Bridge would open up a sinister trail of seemingly unconnected events.

Events which were to culminate in one of the most baffling and personal dilemmas of his career, and a series of crimes which had tragic and far-reaching repercussions several years later.

Faro was to represent the Edinburgh City Police at the funeral in Angus of a former colleague. Will Gray had died in retirement at the ripe old age of ninety and although funerals were sober, sad occasions, he was almost looking forward to this one. In addition to the unique chance of renewing auld acquaintance over nostalgic drams with old chums, it also provided an excuse to visit his stepson.

9 Sheridan Place, Edinburgh, seemed strangely silent without Vince. Faro had ample opportunity to consider the future of the home they had shared until recently. He was increasingly aware of how his footsteps echoed on stairs and through empty rooms meant for a family of children and servants, mocked and reproached one solitary widower.

The truth was undeniable but less than pleasant. The handsome villa in the expanding suburb of Newington was far too big for him since Dr Vincent Beaumarcher Laurie was now resident doctor to the ever expanding firm of Deane Enterprises in Dundee. And Deane's had triumphantly netted, against fierce competition, the building materials contract for the bridge over the River Tay.

In the two months since his stepson's departure, Faro realised how much he had come to depend on the arrival of the postman and Mrs Brook's delivery of the morning mail to his study. In fact, he prided himself that he could deduce from her footsteps, brisk or tardy, whether or not she carried that eagerly awaited letter.

His hopes were mostly shattered. Vince was an indifferent correspondent at the best of times but Faro tempered disappointment with a ready excuse. Of course, the lad's present hectic employment allowed him no idle time for letter-writing.

Faro sighed. Vince might well be far too busy, but not so himself. That spring had been remarkable for a particularly dull patch in the Edinburgh City Police's annals of crime.

There were no really 'interesting' cases on which to flex his powers of deduction. Recent investigations had been limited to petty frauds and the wearisomely repetitive activities of Edinburgh's habitual minor criminals.

Faro's famed and dramatic appearances in the Sheriff Court were required merely to identify witnesses while he secretly longed for action, for the chase and duel to the death with dangerous opponents worthy of his skill. A little ashamed to admit that he was ill-adapted to the tranquil life he had so often longed for in times of danger, Faro discovered that peace for him spelt only monotony and boredom.

Was he growing old? he thought nervously. Were these the normal reactions of a man not much past forty? Failing completely to suppress a wistful longing for the faces of his old adversaries, he wondered where they were now. Had they been converted to good deeds and growing flowers in peaceful tranquility?

And Faro was uneasily aware that unless eyes and ears

10

were constantly alert and watchful for clues and suspects, that extra sense developed by more than twenty years with the City Police would atrophy. Detective Inspector Jeremy Faro would then be of no more use than a newly recruited junior constable.

Preparing to leave Edinburgh for the funeral in the Angus village of Errol, Faro requested a few extra days' leave, partly for the arduous train journey involved and also to visit Dundee. There he hoped to surprise Vince with his unexpected appearance.

His arrangements almost complete, he encountered a breathless Mrs Brook panting upstairs and dramatically flourishing a letter.

'It's from him, sir. It's from the dear lad – at last.'

Thanking her, Faro eagerly tore open the letter. The handwriting was familiar but almost completely illegible. Vince, it appeared, had succumbed to the doctor's pride and privilege of writing that not a soul could read. With a sigh, however, not altogether unpleasurable, Faro sat down to decipher the contents.

'My dear Stepfather,' he read, 'prepare yourself for a surprise, perhaps even a shock.' And in bold capitals heavily underlined: 'I AM ALMOST A MARRIED MAN.' The words leaped out at Faro and he read them twice over before proceeding.

There now, Stepfather, just as you predicted, I have met the girl of my dreams. I love and am loved and we are to marry as soon as her grandfather (and guardian) gives permission as she is still but twenty.

Most revered and devoted Stepfather, I beg of you to prepare to receive a stepdaughter-in-law who will in every conceivable way measure up to your desires for my happiness. And one who having heard much about you, longs above all things to make your acquaintance at the very earliest.

I would most earnestly wish this to be before our

11

wedding and would bring her to you but, alas, we can ill afford the time with many arrangements on hand. May we therefore beg that you pay us a visit as soon as is convenient and give us a father's blessing.

I am, as ever, Your obedient and affectionate Step-son,

Vincent B. Laurie.

Having carefully reread the letter several times, Faro discovered that his first feelings of delight were now mingled with faint irritation that in a matter of such concern and importance, Vince had imparted so little information.

Why, he had not even remembered to include his fiancée's name. Typical of the lad, of course.

With a fond smile, Faro laid the letter aside. This news, so totally unexpected, was good indeed, the very best in all the world. He had always believed that Vince (the invincible where matrimony was concerned) would sooner or later fall in love.

He sighed. His dearest wish for the lad had been granted but there was an obverse side to this good fortune which affected him personally. The camaraderie of their bachelor estate, the companionship of father and son must henceforth take a minor rôle in this new scheme of things.

He closed his mind to such unworthy thoughts, and looking around, nodded vigorously. How strange the coincidence of his decision that the house was no longer suitable. Almost as if that keen extra sense which was at once the plague and blessing of his life had been preparing him for the inevitable changes which must come about with Vince's marriage.

'Time to move on, old chap. A new wife, however charming and well-disposed, is not going to want a police-man stepfather living in the house with them.'

At least this house he had grown to love so well would be saved from a sale to strangers. Indeed he hoped it would now revert to the original purpose the builder had in mind. No doubt in due time Vince and his bride would fill these empty rooms with the laughter of children and the bustle of servants.

'And about time. That's what houses are for,' said Mrs Brook, jubilantly echoing his own thoughts when he rushed downstairs to the kitchen to share this joyful news over a glass of her favourite port.

Even as they talked, he could see she was making her own plans, extending her duties as the efficient housekeeper she had proved to be by engaging extra servants. At this stage he would not spoil her innocent pleasure with the information that although she might well continue to reign over 9 Sheridan Place, he would no longer be her employer.

Knowing that Vince would hotly disapprove, Faro decided to keep an eye open for a small apartment nearer the Central Office. If he looked sharp about it, then he might be able to present the newly-weds with a *fait accompli* when they returned from their honeymoon, thus saving Vince any protest or his bride any embarrassment.

Leaving the house, he closed the front door and looked sadly at the place which until recently bore the brass plate: 'Dr Vincent Beaumarcher Laurie, General Practitioner in Family Medicine'.

They had hung it together on Vince's twenty-first birthday when after a term with the police surgeon he had hoped to set up his surgery in the ground floor rooms. Alas, he had tried but with so little successs that without his stepfather's support, the spectacle of starvation would have loomed large.

The suburbs of Newington and Grange on the sunny southern slopes of the city had become increasingly popular with a new and prosperous merchant and professional class. In such a community, well supplied with physicians, Dr Laurie suffered from two drawbacks. He looked uncommonly young for his age with his head of blonde curls and light build. Time would take care of that, of course, but the main trouble was that he was unmarried.

The area attracted large well-off families, modest matrons who required cosy middle-aged doctors in whom to confide their medical problems and to look after them in childbirth. It was now *de rigueur* in this new middle class to have one's own physician in attendance at the accouchement instead of the friendly neighbour who in the poorer areas acted as midwife.

Vince's own mother had died of childbed fever taking with her the newborn son Faro had craved. He never ceased to mourn her and the fatal risks and frequent deaths of women in childbirth had been one of the main reasons for Vince's choice of a medical career.

He adored his two little stepsisters, Faro's daughters Rose and Emily, who lived in Orkney with their grand-mother and Faro had long ago decided that his stepson's natural ability to gain the trust of children allied with a sharp insight into how their minds worked, might prove invaluable for an unmarried family physician.

Vince's boast since undergraduate days had been 'he who travels fastest travels alone'. With his sights long set on becoming 'Queen's physician' perhaps that love of children would be his sole purpose in eventually marrying at all.

Heads of houses, however, gentlemen if not by birth then by achievement, considered it indelicate, hardly respectable, to have their daughters intimately examined, those pains peculiar to young unmarried ladies discussed and investigated by doctors who looked no older or more reliable than their own young bachelor sons.

Vince was also painfully aware that his background as assistant to the police surgeon was not perhaps the happiest recommendation for dealing with genteel fami-lies. The cutting up of corpses, as the general public saw his activities, suggested a lack-lustre approach to family medicine.

'Since all his previous patients have been dead ones,' as one of his well-meaning patients somewhat tactlessly put it.

Sobered and dismayed by the failure of his practice, Vince had taken the appointment at Deane's Dundee factory with cheerful courage.

Now his unexpected and exciting news seemed in keeping with the warm sunshine and the awakening of lifeless branches in a positive bridal display of blossom. Faro's spirits were again lifted by that joy of renewal in the earth's yearly resurrection which even the prospects of the daunting journey ahead did not immediately quell.

As the crow flies, only forty-six miles separated Edinburgh from Dundee, a journey that should have been a mere bagatelle for a Britain whose web of railroads made accessible distant towns and opened up new opportunities for the labouring classes. Now men could seek employment further afield than the restrictions imposed by walking distances from their own tiny villages.

In the case of Edinburgh and Dundee, however, the deceptively short distance was hampered by the two wide estuaries of Forth and Tay. And their as yet unspanned waters, to be crossed by ferry, turned what should have been a delightful and invigorating prospect of travelling by train at a thrilling thirty miles an hour into the vast proportions of a nightmare.

This was no journey to be undertaken frequently or by busy men thought Faro as he left Sheridan Place at dawn and walked briskly down the Pleasance towards Waverley Station.

With what seemed to intending passengers uncommonly like adding insult to injury, the North British Railway Company ran their best train of the day at 6.25 a.m. According to the timetable it took three hours and twelve minutes.

But that was in only the most favourable weather conditions. In point of fact, the journey could and almost always did take considerably longer. In winter, or in summer storm, the uneasy waters of Forth and Tay stirred angrily thereby causing delays, additional misery and acute discomfort to passengers.

As a stiff wind buffeted him over Waverley Bridge, Faro considered with some apprehension the wild clouds screening a reluctant sunrise. No doubt a gloomy prophecy for a journey even less agreeable than previous experiences which, like painful toothache, he preferred not to dwell upon.

Taking his place in the fireless buffet room of the station among the shivering group of passengers, all valiantly grasping steaming hot cups of coffee which warmed icy hands but had little in the way of taste as commendation, he was told that the train was late.

Frustration and impatience at this stage of the journey boded ill and Faro bitterly regretted his lack of time and forewarning to take the ship overnight from Leith. This was his normal method of travel when occasion led him to the north-east coast of Scotland. Even with his abominable tendency to seasickness, it still remained the happier alternative.

The train arrived at last. 'Engine trouble,' grumbled the porter.

Now mauve in countenance, chilled to the bone, the passengers struggled aboard with their luggage only to find themselves considerably worse off than before. The carriages lacked any internal heating and the train trailed two odorous fish trucks.

Travelling through the suburbs of Edinburgh, occasionally alerting the sleeping occupants with a shrill hoot, the train arrived at Granton-on-Forth, where everyone disembarked and boarded the ferry.

Its appearance was at first sight consoling, low in the hull with beating paddles on either side, high slender smoke-stacks and raking masts. A graceful boat indeed, resting lightly on the water but as the stiff gale, white-lacing the waves, set upon them amidships, the passengers, Faro included, were soon taking refuge against the bulkheads where they wrestled with the urgent demands of heaving stomachs.

Faro was in difficulties. The din of paddles made his head ache and the presence close at hand of fish 'fresh that morning' but already succumbing to speedy decay was extremely offensive.

The short journey across the Firth of Forth seemed abominably long; his discomfort acute, he was grateful to see dry land at Burntisland. There he joined the general pandemonium to seize a seat on the train which would carry them the further thirty-six miles to the south side of the Tay estuary. Taking careful note of how the wind was blowing, he wisely chose a seat facing away from the billowing clouds of smoke and cinder.

Fascinated as he usually was by guessing the character and occupation of his fellow-passengers, the four who shared his compartment were readily dismissed as a young wife with a snivelling child and her volatile mother, plus an elderly clergyman. Their characters and conversation left little room for speculation or the scent of mystery.

An inveterate gazer-out-of-windows, he was further frustrated as the Kingdom of Fife was blanketed by heavy mist, rendering visibility negligible. Disappointed that spring had chosen this moment for a bleak return to desolation, he prepared to pass the time as agreeably as possible. With the help of one of his favourite travelling companions, Mr Charles Dickens, he applied himself once again to his current reading: *The Mystery of Edwin Drood*.

The tedium at last over, he greeted with relief the station at Newport where another ferry-boat now waited to carry them across the Tay. Relieved that the weather had improved enough to make their destination visible, he observed the ancient castle at Broughty Ferry bathed in a flicker of sunlight.

Soon he would be meeting Vince and his bride-to-be. But before that, here was what the newspapers called 'one

17

of the marvels of the modern world, the Bridge across the River Tay'.

It was, he decided, something of a disappointment. Marked by half-finished piers on either side of the estuary, it resembled nothing more than a gigantic loosely-knitted iron ribbon with ends trailing into the water.

Boarding the ferry, the air was clouded by the glow and smoke belch of nearby foundries. As they drifted into the water, their ears were assaulted by the thunderous beat of the pile-drivers while their eyes smarted from the furnaces' acrid fumes.

Observing this scene of high activity, Faro thought it odd that there had been so little progress to show on the bridge for two years' work. Even making allowances for marvels of engineering well beyond his comprehension, he could not visualise that frail structure supporting anything as robust and substantial as a railway train.

And he remembered that when the bridge was being planned, an old man, an apple-grower famous for his true prophecies as the Seer of Gourdiehill, had seen its completion and downfall.

'This rainbow bridge', Patrick Matthews had called it, and on his deathbed he had had a final terrible vision: 'A great wind will wrench at the high girders, crushing the bridge and a heavy passenger train with the whole of the passengers will be killed.'

A black cloud blotted out the sunlight, shrouding the half-finished bridge in sudden gloom.

Faro shivered, remembering the last words of the Seer's prophecy: 'The eels will come to gloat in delight over the horrible wreck and banquet.'

Chapter Two

At Faro's side on the ferry, the minister who had spent most of the train journey sleeping heavily had regained animation:

'Ah, sir, we are now witnessing the famed Thomas Bouch's creation. He has travelled a long way from aqueducts to the longest bridge in the world.'

As he gazed at the massive iron structures, Faro shrugged aside his misgivings. 'There is a saying that children and fools should never see things half completed.'

'Oh ye of little faith,' quoted the minister with a smile and a reproachful nod. 'Think what a difference it will make to our travel and to our prosperity. God be praised that man's achievement will mean an end to all that wearisome changing of trains and ferries,' he added fervently.

'Amen to that, sir.'

The minister waved a hand in the direction of one of the high girders. 'Astonishing, is it not? Why, the novel concept of weaving iron and masonry through two miles of air and water has delighted the whole of Scotland. They can talk of nothing else.'

'Not only in Scotland, sir. The popular press would have us believe that the idea of bridging the Tay has set fire to the nation's imagination. In London, I understand, folks believe that all that is new and good and noble in this century of scientific endeavour must be done by Englishmen.'

The minister gave him a hard look. 'Indeed, sir, we are

19

living in an age of new gods and although our people sneer at the ignorant superstitions of poor African savages and those other races we are bringing to civilisation by God's word, they see no cause for dismay in the blind trust they are placing in their own industrial witch-doctors.'

Awaiting Faro's nod of approval, he added proudly, 'I am glad you agree, sir, for that was the subject of my sermon in Edinburgh from which I am newly returned.'

It seemed that having detected a sympathetic ear and a captive audience, the minister was eager to deliver that sermon once again. However, before he could utter more than a philosophical sentence or two, he was forestalled by the rapid approach of the quayside at Broughty Ferry where a band of raggedy children shrilly assailled them with demands for ha'pennies and sweeties.

'Get along with you,' said the minister indignantly. Turning to Faro he added by way of apology, 'They mean no harm, but they so enjoy tormenting strangers.'

'Then let us make this a memorable day for them,' said Faro good-humouredly. Digging into his pockets he threw a handful of coins which were pounced upon with noisy delight and even some thanks in his direction.

'You spoil them with such generosity,' said the minister reproachfully. 'You have children of your own?'

'Yes, sir. Two wee daughters, a little better behaved but with every child's weakness for ha'pennies and sweeties.'

'You are bound for Dundee?' said the minister. 'Ah, then our ways part here. I wish you well, for the worst is over.'

Bidding him good day, Faro boarded the train and ten minutes later he alighted in Dundee Station where the platform soon emptied of passengers.

But of Vince there was no sign.

Now chilled to the bone, Faro paced briskly up and down in a vain attempt to restore his circulation. He was accompanied in this activity by a middle-aged man who walked back and forth with the impatient angry look of one who had just missed his train.

Raising his hat politely, Faro asked, 'Are you awaiting the Perth train, sir?'

The man merely scowled and, biting his lips, continued his perambulation fast enough to discourage further conversation. His occasional pauses were merely to glare across at the unfinished piers of what would some day be the Tay Bridge.

Faro, who considered such behaviour extremely boorish, again consulted the timetable outside the stationmaster's office. He had hoped to spend an hour with Vince before the arrival of his train for Errol but as the minutes ticked away, he was seized by a sudden foreboding.

The lad should have had his telegraph. So where in the world was he?

Then a sudden diversion swept all other thoughts from his mind. A train had arrived from Aberdeen and as it emptied, the pacing man came leaping forward to grapple with a youngish fellow who had descended from first class.

Holding him in a fierce grip, he forced him to the very edge of the platform, so that he tottered unsteadily above the rails.

'Murderer,' shouted the older man. 'Vile murderer. I ought to push you under the next train and let it decapitate you. For that is all you deserve, after what you did to my lad.'

The youngish man had been taken by surprise. He could do nothing but gasp, struggle feebly and call for help.

Faro and the porter dashed to his assistance but the older man was strong and for several dizzy seconds the four trembled above the rails, surging back and forth in a wild dance. At last they succeeded in separating the two men.

'Thank you, sir, for you intervention.'

The younger man would have been handsome but for a tight closed-in look about the eyes and mouth. It added

21

considerably to his thirty-odd years. 'This madman means my death.'

'Aye, that I do. And never forget it. This is our second encounter, Wilfred Deane, and next time I swear to God I will kill you, as you killed my poor laddie.'

'What's happening? What's going on here?' The station-master emerged to see what all the noise was about. 'Oh, it's you again, is it, McGowan? I've warned you before.'

A uniformed coachman appeared through the barrier and rushed to Deane murmuring apologies and concern.

'Yes, damn you, you should have been here to meet me on time. I might have been killed.'

'That one was threatening to murder your master,' said the porter.

'Murder, is it?' said the station-master. 'Hold him fast, Jim. It's the police for you, my man. Upsetting my passengers.' And to Deane, 'My apologies, sir. You have my assurances – it won't happen again, sir.'

'I sincerely hope not. It will cost you your job next time, Station-master. Pray bear that in mind. You are responsible for the conduct and safety of fare-paying passengers and for keeping madmen away from your platform.'

The station-master, nonplussed, grew red in the face with anger and embarrassment. 'If this gentleman – you, sir,' he said indicating Faro – 'will kindly assist me in restraining McGowan, I will send Jim for the police.'

Mollified, the youngish man bowed stiffly. 'See to it, Station-master.' And dusting down his sleeves as if to remove all traces of the incident he hurried the coachman towards the exit.

Watching them leave, the station-master said: 'Off you go, Jim.'

McGowan, held captive, suddenly began to weep in a helpless broken way, a weakness so out of keeping with his former belligerence that Faro called to the departing

22

porter: 'Wait,' and to the station-master: 'It so happens that I am a policeman.'

'Are you indeed?' The station-master stared at him doubtfully. 'You don't look like one, if you'll forgive me saying so,' he added in tones of ill-concealed sarcasm.

Faro drew out his wallet. 'My card, sir.'

The man's eyes bulged as he read. 'Oh, sir, my apologies. Of course I've heard of Detective Inspector Faro. You're quite famous.'

Faro smiled. 'Then perhaps you will trust me to take care of your prisoner.'

'Indeed I will. He won't escape from you.'

McGowan was still weeping abjectly as Faro took his arm gently and led him to the only shelter, a somewhat inhospitable waiting-room. Its only furnishings besides a couple of slatted wooden benches were a few faded posters urging travel by railway. But the alluring sylvan scenes they depicted were not to be found, he suspected, anywhere outside the artist's vivid imagination.

Suddenly McGowan gripped Faro's arm. 'How can I ever thank you, sir. The scandal – after losing our lad – my wife's been in a poor way ever since, and I fear it would have finished her.'

Faro consulted his watch. It seemed unlikely that Vince would appear now. He had some time before his train and he was curious.

'Would you care to tell me about it?'

'You won't let them put me inside, will you, Inspector?'

The man before him seemed less like a potential murderer than anyone he had ever met. 'I don't think that will be necessary.'

'Wilfred Deane murdered my laddie.'

'Is he of the Deane Enterprises family?'

'He is that. He runs the show now that his old grandfather Sir Arnold is past it.'

'I see. Begin at the beginning, if you please, Mr McGowan.'

'We are from the Highlands, Inverness way. I was

23

dominie there and Charlie was our only lad. Twelve years married, we had given up all hope of a family when he was born, the bairn of our old age you might call him. From when he was a wee boy he was clever. We scrimped and saved to put him through the University at St Andrews. He graduated with flying colours a couple of years ago and went to Deane's. He was in their finance department.

'This was right at the beginning of their contract for the Tay Bridge and he seemed to be happy at first, enjoying his work. He married Mary, his childhood sweetheart, and they seemed like two turtle doves.

'Then the last time they came to visit us, he was different. Silent, worried-looking, like he had something on his mind and was about to tell us. A week later, Charlie came alone. The manager of his office, an elderly bachelor called Simms who had been with the firm for years and had been very kind to Charlie and Mary, had been dismissed. Deane's said he was dishonest, but Charlie didn't believe that for a moment. Simms had told him that he had been suspicious of the finances for some time and was carrying on a private investigation into the firm's dealings.'

McGowan paused. 'Those were his exact words. Almost the last words he ever spoke to me and I shall remember them to my dying day.'

As he listened, Faro wondered what on earth had led him to befriend this stranger. The scent of a mystery – or was it instinct, combined with an odd compassion for the bereaved father and a spontaneous dislike of Wilfred Deane?

With a painful sigh, McGowan continued, 'Two days later, we read in the papers that Simms had been visiting the bridge and had been hit by a falling girder. He had died instantly.'

He was silent for a moment before continuing, his eyes welling with tears as he spoke.'We expected Charlie and Mary for supper that night and when they didn't

24

appear, my wife was alarmed and sent me to the office next morning. I was informed that Charlie had failed to show up. I went to their home, but they weren't there. Everything put away neat and tidy, but no papers, nothing personal, not even their wedding photograph.'

He shook his head. 'I didn't want to alarm the wife, she's in poor health as I told you. It was just as if they had gone off on holiday and hadn't told us. I wish to God that had been the way of it. Three days later, the police came and said my laddie's body had been washed up at the Ferry.'

'What about his wife, Mary?'

McGowan looked at him slowly, shook his head. 'She's never been seen again. We've been in touch with her folks, we've notified the police, but it's as if she's vanished from the face of the earth.'

He paused. 'I fear the worst. She's been done away with too.'

'Come now, Mr McGowan, let's not be too hasty in jumping to conclusions.' The policeman in Faro hinted that if murder was involved then it was more likely that young McGowan had done away with his wife and committed suicide, the familiar pattern of the *crime passionel*.

As if he read Faro's thoughts, McGowan leaped to his feet. 'Hasty, is it? My son was a good Catholic, human life was sacred to him. His own and anyone else's. As for Simms, the way I look at it, his accident was arranged too, like my laddie's. They both died because of what Simms had found out. And Wilfred Deane murdered them.'

It was a shocking story. Though exaggerated by McGowan's despair, Faro wondered if there might be some grain of truth in it.

'You can easily find out if I'm speaking the truth, Inspector, the police at Dundee have all the details.'

Faro nodded vigorously. 'I will certainly do that. You have my word, Mr McGowan.' And as a shrill whistle indicated the arrival of the Perth train. 'Not that I don't believe you,' he added hastily, 'rather that

I do and I want to help you if I possibly can. Let me have your address.' Watching McGowan scribble it on a piece of paper, Faro said: 'I will do this on one condition only.'

'And what is that, Inspector? I have very little money.'

'I don't want your money. Only your solemn promise that you will refrain from molesting Wilfred Deane any further. For if you are arrested and charged, it will be a serious offence and I cannot guarantee to help you. Do you understand?'

McGowan smiled and held out his hand. 'I give you my word, the solemn oath of a Highland gentleman. I swear to God that I will never again take the law into my own hands regarding Wilfred Deane. I leave it to the Almighty – and you, sir, to deliver him to justice.'

As Faro emerged on to the platform, McGowan saluted him; 'I will take my leave by the side gate,' he whispered. 'I would rather not encounter the station-master alone.' And as the Perth train steamed in: 'I can never thank you enough, Inspector. You have given me new hope.'

Searching the platform with one last despairing glance for Vince, Faro nodded briefly and boarded the train. Settling back in his seat, he realised that McGowan's fearful story had put him in the right state of mind to conjure up a whole volume of sinister reasons for his stepson's non-arrival.

Vince was always so reliable. Why then had he failed to meet the train?

The guard had already waved his flag when a young lad came panting along the platform yelling: 'Mr Faro? Mr Faro?'

Faro leaned out of the carriage. 'Over here.'

The train was gathering steam. 'I have a message for you. From Dundee,' he shouted breathlessly, thrusting a piece of paper into Faro's hand. 'There's been an accident.'

Chapter Three

There was no possibility of leaving the train now.

Faro sank back into his seat and thanked God that the note was scribbled in Vince's familiar hand.

'I am urgently needed at the Infirmary. Will meet you for luncheon tomorrow at the Glamis Hotel (opposite the railway station).'

As the countryside chugged past the windows, Faro felt he had plenty to keep his mind occupied after his conversation with McGowan. He had given his word to the boy's father. Without stirring any troubled waters with the Dundee City Police, he could make a few discreet enquiries into the death of Charlie McGowan, and his young wife's disappearance. He could verify that Simms' death had been accidental.

A strange ugly business, with some decidedly sinister undertones. As the unfinished bridge retreated into the distance, Faro decided that if there was indeed corruption and fraud within Deane Enterprises and they were supplying the building materials, then a lot more lives of innocent unsuspecting people might be at hazard.

The journey to Errol was mercifully short. He was met by Tom Elgin, limping across the platform. A former constable with the Edinburgh City Police, Tom had been injured in a riot in the Grassmarket and no longer fit for active service had returned to Angus to become gamekeeper to the aristocratic family his forebears had served for generations.

To a man whose daily dealings were with violent

death, the passing of a ninety-year-old who slips peace-fully away in his bed at the end of a long and happy life was an occasion for gladness rather than bleak despair.

The wake included a great deal of food and a consid-erable number of drams to speed Will Gray on his way. Truth to tell, Faro was in no fit condition to return to Dundee or anywhere else for that matter, even if a late train had existed. He was readily persuaded to stay the night with Tom.

'The funeral? More like a reunion with old friends,' he told Vince when they met next day in the Glamis Hotel.

'So it would appear,' said Vince whose amused glance took in his stepfather's somewhat shattered appearance. 'Well, I take it that you received my letter,' he added shyly.

'I did indeed. My heartiest congratulations, lad. This is great news.'

'I thought you would be pleased.'

'And when am I to have the pleasure of meeting your fiancée?'

'Even at this moment, she is waiting to receive us. Come along, Stepfather. The hall porter will get us a cab.'

As they waited in the foyer, Vince asked: 'How was your journey from Edinburgh?'

'A nightmare, as usual,' said Faro huffily. 'The sooner they get that bridge finished the better.'

'Oh, we're coming on,' said Vince cheerfully as the cab arrived and from its windows they surveyed the skeleton of the bridge with its still wide central gap.

'Any fool can see that the joining of those two piers from Wormit to Dundee is nowhere in sight,' said Faro. 'They're certainly taking their time about it.'

'Oh, I gather there have been plenty of complications – and still are.'

'Such as?' demanded Faro eagerly.

Vince shrugged. 'Too long to go into at the moment.'

28

'Hmphh,' said Faro and peering out he added: 'Doesn't look very substantial to me.'

Rumours had reached the Central Office and filtered through the popular press of terrible accidents and of the wild war waged between the Caledonian and the North British Railways over monopoly rights.

Tom Elgin had told him that the city of Perth had been far from pleased, jealous that the bridge might diminish their own river trade. And now he had also received, at first hand, hints of sinister goings-on from McGowan.

'Will it ever be strong or safe enough to carry a train, I wonder?'

'Safe as houses or, as they advertise, sound as Deane's,' was Vince's reply. 'The fact that they secured the contract puts a rather different complexion on the matter. Deane's stand for respectability and honest dealings.'

'Sound as Deane's' had been a familiar phrase in Dundee for the past fifty years, ever since Sir Arnold Deane had set a new fashion of combining expertise in finance with compassion for his employees. His boast was: 'We are all brothers here, all one big family.'

'Incidentally, Stepfather, Sir Arnold is a patient of mine,' Vince added casually.

'Congratulations, lad.' And in view of that information, Faro had second thoughts. He would keep McGowan's story to himself meanwhile. Indeed it had become more extraordinary and unbelievable over the last twenty-four hours. Was he wasting his sympathies on a madman?

As if in confirmation of his thoughts Vince said: 'Deane's are into everything these days, Stepfather. Sometimes one would think they had invented the word progress. And the good thing is that in their case, everyone benefits by their prosperity.'

Faro looked out of the window and discovered they were now following the Monifieth Road, alongside the river east of Dundee. On the steep hills rising to the left perched the elegant handsome mansions built by the jute lords.

'Where are we heading, lad?' he demanded curiously.

Vince smiled. 'Deane Hall.'

'*The* Deane Hall?'

'The same,' said Vince with a grin.

Glancing sideways at Vince he noted his air of suppressed excitement. 'Home of the Sir Arnold, Baron of Broughty Ferry, who is a patient of yours?'

'Excellent, Stepfather, excellent,' said Vince.

'Vince, is there something you have forgotten to tell me?'

'Not forgotten, just hadn't time to go into it. Didn't know whether you would approve. Rachel is the Deane heiress—'

'Rachel – the young lady you are to marry?'

'Of course.' Observing his stepfather's expression he added, 'Oh Lord, did I not even tell you her name?'

'You omitted that vital clue. But please proceed . . . '

'Rachel inherits next month when she comes of age. She is Sir Arnold's only grandchild.'

'Well, well, you have done well for yourself, lad. First the resident doctor and then the heiress's husband,' said Faro with a smile.

'It's a family tradition. After all, Sir Arnold's father was a poor Yorkshire lad who came to Scotland and ended up by marrying his boss's daughter, who was also an heiress.'

Faro said nothing and, alarmed by his silence, Vince said hotly: 'If you're thinking it is her money—'

'Of course I'm not, lad—' Observing Vince's dark frown, he added hastily, 'A figure of speech and in my usual bad taste, I'm afraid. The policeman in me sometimes forgets. Do forgive me.'

Vince did so readily. 'Let me tell you, even if Rachel had been the poorest of the workers I have to attend in the factory, I still would want to marry her. She is so beautiful, the loveliest raven black hair, eyes like violets—'

He paused, suddenly embarrassed. 'But you will see for yourself in a few moments. We met one day quite by

30

accident, when I was attending her grandfather . . . '

Faro listened, smiling, delighted by his stepson's happiness but at the same time wondering how on earth the lad was to support an heiress. Certainly not on his salary as resident doctor.

But Vince was no longer aware of reality or indeed of his stepfather's presence. And with compassion Faro recognised that Vince had happily surrendered his grasp of the practicalities of life. Gazing fondly at the lad, he observed him in the throes of that state of temporary insanity which Faro considered, from his own bitter experience, as being 'in love'.

Deane Hall was a mansion with a setting worthy of the Baron of Broughty's rôle in society and commerce. Battlemented, turreted as any castle of old, it overlooked the unfinished piers of the Tay Bridge.

One day, Sir Arnold expected that a fine monument gazing down upon the river would be the city fathers' acknowledgement of his rôle in Dundee's progress and Deane's contribution to the longest bridge in the world. A bridge that would stand for ever, carrying the railway linking the northernmost towns and cities of Scotland with those of the rest of Britain. Most gratifying of all was that this vital link had acquired royal approval, giving her Majesty and the royal families of Europe easy access to Balmoral Castle.

Vince was arguing with the cab driver who was unwilling to tackle the last hundred yards of almost vertical climb from the ornate gates to the front door. Receiving his fare he dismissed his passengers brusquely and drove off leaving them to puff up the steep drive.

Faro sighed. 'Times have indeed changed. One would imagine he was doing us a great favour, bringing us here at all.'

'It's going down rather than up they really fear, Stepfather. They reckon that wealthy folk like the Baron who choose to live on inaccessible hilltops can afford their own sturdy carriages to bring up their affluent guests.

31

Besides the exercise will do us good,' he added with a cheerful grin.

'Don't you think I get enough of that every day in Edinburgh?' grumbled Faro.

The driveway emerged on to a terrace which again afforded a panoramic view of the hills of Fife. The university town of St Andrews with its spires was minutely visible and to the west the faint undulating slopes of the Grampian Mountains.

Faro whistled. 'Well, that makes it almost worth the climb. What a magnificent landscape.'

'And one which is even better from the drawing room and the upstairs windows.'

Narrowing his eyes, Faro said: 'The bridge will certainly look most impressive when it's finished.'

'Sir Arnold is banking on it. He has, I understand, sunk a considerable part of his fortune into the construction. His engineering works supply the nuts and bolts, his weavers supply the cloth for sacking, overalls—'

'Overalls? That is progress indeed.'

'He firmly believes in attending to the needs and comfort as well as the safety of his workers. They eat a good nourishing meal once a day too, compliments of the firm. A splendid canteen, I can assure you and one I am often very grateful to patronise.'

'Less fortunate workers must envy them. Sounds quite idyllic.'

Vince frowned. 'It does – but alas, progress has a knack, which I'm sure you've noticed, of crushing the helpless who cannot keep up with it.'

'How so?' asked Faro as they climbed an imposing set of stone steps guarded by two ferocious heraldic lions.

'The working conditions give me cause for concern. Small wonder they need a resident doctor,' whispered Vince as he rang the doorbell. 'I am constantly dealing with terrible – and, I feel, quite unnecessary – accidents and maimings. The men blame shoddy materials and unsafe conditions of work. Some have even tried, poor

32

beggars, or their dependants have tried, to bring Deane's to court.' He laughed grimly. 'But Wilfred is too smart for them.'

'Wilfred?'

'Sir Arnold's second cousin. He's a lot younger, of course.'

So that was the Wilfred Deane who had been set upon by McGowan.

The door was opened by a butler. 'Dr Laurie to see Miss Deane, if you please.'

'Are you expected, sir?'

'No, I am not. But here is my card – and my step-father's.'

Faro produced his card which the butler consulted gravely before transferring it to the silver tray. 'If you will be seated, gentlemen, I will see if Miss Deane is at home to receive you.'

As they waited, Faro marvelled at this replica of a vast medieval hall. Ghostly suits of armour, ancient flags and every degree of opulence surrounded them. A huge log fire burned in a stone fireplace, wastefully consuming what looked like whole trees to keep warm no one in particular.

Occasionally he glanced at his stepson's excited face, flushed and smiling, a lover's face of anticipation and longing as he tapped his foot impatiently.

Faro meanwhile tried to suppress his own anxieties. A veritable parade of dismal practical questions surged through his mind, concerning Vince's ability to support a wife accustomed to such a life-style as that in evidence.

The butler returned, carrying his silver tray which still bore their cards. 'I regret, gentlemen, that Miss Deane is not at home.'

'You mean she is out?' said Vince in tones of surprise.

'I mean, sir, that she is not at home,' the butler replied carefully.

'Look, you know me. I am Sir Arnold's physician,' said Vince.

The butler's face was impassive. 'Is it then Sir Arnold you wish to see, sir?'

'No,' said Vince desperately. 'Look, would you please tell Rach— Miss Deane, Dr Laurie is here to see her. And that I have brought my stepfather to meet her.'

The butler's face was impassive as he ushered them politely but firmly towards the front door. 'Perhaps you would be so good as to leave a message, sir. I will see that it is delivered to Miss Deane at the very earliest.'

'Tell her I will call again. Tomorrow afternoon at three thirty.'

'Very well, sir. Good day.'

As they walked down the drive Vince, bewildered and mutinous, wore an expression Faro recalled from his difficult early years, when deprived of a particularly toothsome treat, or dragged unwillingly from a child's tea-party.

'Never mind, lad. She probably forgot all about it.'

Vince seized on his words eagerly. 'That's it exactly, Stepfather. Such a commitment of social engagements. The mind positively reels. I did tell her when you were arriving, but you know what girls are like, with milliners and dressmakers, and friends for ever calling and leaving cards . . . '

Faro listened patiently, but he wasn't particularly impressed or convinced. He had seen something that his stepson in his preoccupation had mercifully missed.

As they walked across the gravel towards the drive, he had turned to look back at the house. At one of the grand windows upstairs a girl with raven black hair, most elegantly attired in afternoon dress, was watching them leave. As she caught his curious gaze, she stepped back hastily, but Faro had not the least doubt from Vince's description that the watcher was Miss Rachel Deane.

And that sight disturbed him exceedingly.

34

Chapter Four

As they walked back down the hill Vince continued to provide perfectly valid reasons, which even Faro could not fault, for Rachel Deane's non-appearance.

At last they reached Paton's Lane, a mean street of high and gloomy tenements. On the very edge of Magdalen Green its prospects were made marginally more dismal by the shadow and noisy sounds of activity drifting from the direction of the unfinished bridge.

'Here we are, Stepfather.'

Faro followed Vince into a narrow close, up a dark and dank stone stair to the third floor where the odorous smells became unmistakably boiled cabbage. At the end of a chilly dark passage Vince opened a door and for a moment Faro toyed with the notion that his stepson was visiting a sick patient and had absent-mindedly forgotten to inform him.

Until he announced: 'Home at last.'

If this was home, then Faro was aghast. An iron bedstead, a chair and table which by the amount of papers and writing materials also served as a desk, a crude shelf above containing medical books. A press stood on a sadly uneven floor whose bare boards were visible through an inadequate strip of cracked and faded linoleum.

Totally unable to conceal his feelings, Faro asked: 'Lad, are you so short of cash? You had but to ask—'

Vince drew himself up proudly. 'Never, Stepfather. Never again. I intend to make my way in the world alone. It is about time and I cannot sponge on you for ever. You have done more than enough for me.'

'There's no talk of sponging among kin – you know better than that, you're my lad – whatever I own is yours, or will be some day.' He made a weary gesture round the room. 'To think of you living in such squalor. Surely you could have found yourself some respectable private lodging? In a better part of the town,' he added indignantly.

'I could indeed, but by my reckoning, a doctor if he is to be any good at all, should be on hand when his patients need him and I couldn't be closer to mine. A workers' doctor must understand the needs of the men – and women – he has chosen to serve. I have a proper fully-equipped surgery and consulting room in the factory of course.'

At his stepfather's dour expression, he smiled wryly: 'I assure you that you need have no fears on the score of respectability. The McGonagalls are paragons. Besides,' he went on reassuringly, moving the lace curtain aside, 'look out there. Is that not the most exciting prospect?'

Before them stretched the impressive but distinctly unbeautiful panorama of the bridge. The height of skeletal iron piers threatened to dwarf everything in the immediate vicinity, but it too had become a pale ghost, almost obliterated by a monstrous cloud of fine dust from foundry chimneys.

On ground level far below, all footpaths had ceased to exist, vanishing under the mud stirred everywhere by bands of navvies striving to connect roads with the landfalls, an activity accompanied by an ear-splitting din. The blast of explosives shook the room in which they stood, vying with the incessant rhythm of rivets driven home against steel girders while the creak of cranes elevating materials skyward added their unlovely screech to the scene.

'Behold,' said Vince proudly, 'history in the making. And that is the important thing, Stepfather.'

'That's all very well. But I don't think I'd wish to have the bridge's presence outside my window, so to speak, a constant companion night and day.'

His weary glance took in the contents of the room. 'At least it looks clean enough,' he conceded. For the shabby wood gleamed, the oilcloth sparkled, and the room smelt distinctly of polish.

'Of course it is. That bed is spotless. Mrs Mac is very particular, changes the sheets every week.'

Faro found little consolation in such an assurance as the pleasant Edinburgh house Vince had left loomed in his mind, a modest paradise in comparison.

Knowing that argument was useless, he said weakly, 'I'd just like to see you with more comfortable lodgings. You gave me to understand that Deane's were paying a good salary.'

'Moderately good, Stepfather, considering what my earnings were in Sheridan Place,' Vince added bitterly. 'But I have another reason for living frugally at present. Don't you see, by staying here I can put by a little every week, which I will need of course, once Rachel and I are married.'

Faro was appalled. Shock at finding his stepson living in this wretched room had momentarily put out of his head that Vince was to marry Deane's heiress. God in heaven, how could the lad be so blind, remembering the splendour they had glimpsed, the mock-medieval hall, every sign of wealth and comfort.

Any comparison between Rachel Deane's home and this squalid lodging was not only unimaginable but obscene.

'Has Miss Deane visited you here?' he asked idly.

'Please call her Rachel, Stepfather. There has been no occasion for her to do so. And until the engagement is formally announced it would not be proper—'

Faro was spared any further comment as an infant wailed somewhere nearby. Vince went over and opened the door. The cries grew louder.

37

'That's the McGonagall baby.' Vince listened and was reassured by rapid footsteps. 'Mrs McGonagall isn't far away.'

Smiling at Faro, he continued, 'That was my other reason for choosing this lodging. The McGonagall's have six children, steps of stairs you might say, as well as an orphaned cousin from Ireland. William, the husband, is a weaver with Deane's but he has aspirations to being an actor – a tragedian, he prefers to call himself. I attended him – just a minor accident with one of the machines – and he asked me to look at Jean, Mrs Mac, who had bronchitis.

'Well, when I came along I saw what a struggle they had. She's from Edinburgh, does some cleaning to make ends meet. Funny, in a way she reminded me of our dear Mrs Brook – same voice, you know, and an absolutely splendid cook.'

Vince paused awaiting his stepfather's approval. When Faro remained silent, he added: 'I do think I was a little homesick and when she told me she had a spare room, I said yes, I would take it. She was so grateful, said I was offering far more than it was worth. But I feel better about it, helping a family with my little rent.'

Faro suppressed any adverse comment. There was no dealing with a philanthropic Vince. Once his thoughts of chivalry were aroused, no knight of old in shining armour could have fought more vigorously for a lost cause.

And this particular lost cause, thought Faro, was one without any real solution, with Deane's good works just one drop in an ocean of grim poverty. Poverty so deep-rooted he did not see the much-vaunted building of the Tay Bridge bringing any substantial relief, lining as it would only the pockets of its wealthy shareholders.

As for the common man, he would find other bridges, other roads to build, his life of grime and hardship remaining virtually unchanged.

'There is a room for you, Stepfather, next door. Would

you like to see it? Of course, if it isn't good enough and you don't like it, you can go to a hotel.'

Faro followed him reluctantly. As he expected, the room was almost identical except for touches here and there of a feminine presence.

'This belongs to Kathleen, the cousin from Ireland. Came over when her mother died. Thought the streets of Dundee were paved with gold. Willie adores her and had aspirations for her to be an actress, too. Apparently she isn't quite ready for Shakespeare, so he got her a job in the factory.'

'Is she not needing this room?'

Vince frowned. 'You'll like this, Stepfather. Sounds exactly like one of your baffling mysteries. Seems she went out to work one day with her friend Polly – they shared this room. That's weeks ago and no one's seen them since.'

Sounds outside the door, a man's voice calculated to carry a great distance and enthrall an audience, announced the arrival of William McGonagall, even before Vince's smile confirmed that his landlord had returned home.

'You'll like McGonagall, he's a grand old chap, very colourful – shares your passion for the Bard,' he whispered opening the door.

The figure who appeared was slightly unreal. Below middle height, sturdily built, melancholy dark eyes gazing from a pale face, framed by black shoulder-length curls under a wide-brimmed hat, the kind worn by priests. His frock-coat, once black but still impressive despite its green tinged antiquity, was an unlikely choice for a worker in the weaving factory.

Seeing Vince, he rushed forward hand outstretched: 'Dear lad, dear lad. How goes it with you?' And turning to Faro, he took off his hat in a sweeping gesture which matched the theatrical bow.

'And you, sir, must be Dr Laurie's famous stepfather, the Chief Inspector.' As they shook hands he regarded

39

Faro shrewdly. 'Your activities in the realms of criminology are well known to me. My sister-in-law who inhabits your fair city of Edinburgh has mentioned your name.' Another bow: 'Allow me to present my card and credentials, sir.' Faro glanced in some surprise at the small package. 'If you would care to attend this evening's performance of *Macbeth*, there are two free tickets. The noble Inspector's presence would add lustre to your humble servant's performance.'

Faro suppressed a smile, for there was nothing at all humble in this extraordinary man with the booming voice and eccentric garb.

Leaning forward confidentially, McGonagall placed a hand on his arm and his face now serious, he continued: 'Indeed, I am delighted to make your acquaintance. Fate must have sent you to Dundee at this time,' he added gloomily and looking over his shoulder, he gestured towards the room at the end of the corridor.

'But let us be comfortable, for I have a melancholy tale to unfold. If you will be so good as to follow me into our humble kitchen, Mrs M will provide us with refreshment.'

Jean McGonagall hastily buttoned up her gown as the men entered and laid the now sleepy baby in a somewhat battered cradle. After quickly introducing her to Faro, McGonagall said in a lordly manner:

'And now, be so good as to provide sustenance for these gentlemen.'

Faro took the proffered seat in one of the rickety chairs by the side of a blackleaded and highly polished steel range with ashpan and fender. The room was humble indeed, shabby but again well cared for within its limits. Four wooden kitchen chairs and a large scrubbed wooden table occupied the centre floor, while a recess held a double bed. Lace curtains adorned the one solitary window above a sink with well-polished brass tap.

Dominating the mantelpiece, a pendulum clock with

ferocious tick, a brass tea caddy, and a pair of china dogs. Opposite, a dresser displayed a variety of unmatching china teacups and plates, interspersed with photographs. Mostly of McGonagall, presumably in costume from his leading Shakespearean rôles.

Faro was suddenly aware that McGonagall was addressing him.

'As I remarked earlier, sir, it is fortuitous indeed that you should be visiting Dundee at this time. Dr Laurie may have told you that my niece and her young friend disappeared—'

'Willie,' said Jean chidingly. 'They didn't disappear. You are too dramatic, dear. We had a postcard that they had found employment with a milliner's in Regent Street. They only went to London to improve their prospects,' she added apologetically.

'Poor Polly certainly did not improve hers,' said William heavily. When his wife gave a startled 'Oh!' he withdrew a piece of newspaper from his pocket and spread it on the table.

'You remember reading in the newspaper two days ago that the body of an unknown young woman had been recovered from the Tay – a suspected suicide—'

'Oh dear God, not our Kathleen—'

'No, woman, not Kathleen,' McGonagall replied impatiently, turning to Faro. 'If I had not been a tragedian I think I would have made an excellent detective—'

'For God's sake get on with it, Willie,' cried his wife, nervously twisting the ends of her apron. 'If it isn't Kathleen, who is it?'

'Hear me out, woman, for pity's sake. Where was I? Oh yes, I have already indicated that I have a naturally curious nature and ever since the two girls disappeared, I have been keeping a watchful eye on the newspapers and have made it my business to keep the police informed for their missing persons files—'

'You never told me,' was the reproachful cry from his wife.

41

'I did not want to alarm you unnecessarily, especially when you seemed quite content to believe they were bettering themselves in London.'

He sighed and winked at the two men. 'I am a little more worldly-wise than Mrs McGonagall, gentlemen, and when I read of this apparent suicide I decided to give the matter my personal attention.'

Another dramatic pause while he drank deep. Jean McGonagall had set before the company enamel cups of bitter black tea, thereby providing Faro with some difficulties. This he guessed was Irish tea, beloved of the navvies, for even the tough Edinburgh constables didn't make it this strong in the Central Office.

McGonagall looked at each of his small audience in turn before proceeding. 'I have newly returned from the police station—'

'It is Polly, isn't it?' said Jean with a sob.

He nodded. 'Sadly, my dear, it is Polly. I was able to identify her body in the mortuary. There is no doubt about it.'

With a glance at his wife who was now weeping noisily, he drew them aside. 'And now do you get my drift, gentlemen? The two girls were inseparable, so where in dear God's name – is our Kathleen?'

Stretching over to the mantelpiece, he took down a picture postcard of Trafalgar Square and studied it carefully. 'The question remains, sirs, is she still in this milliner's shop in Regent Street?'

'May I see?' Faro was more interested in the postmark than the cramped ill-written message. But as was so often the case when such matters were of crucial importance, the date was completely illegible.

Jean McGonagall, drying her eyes, snatched up a rather blurred photograph from the dresser. The girl smiling coyly through a cloud of blonde curls was little more than a child. 'This is our Kathleen.'

'Bonny lass, she is,' said McGonagall proudly.

'She is indeed,' said Faro.

McGonagall nodded. 'Hasn't changed very much since that was taken either, three-four years ago.'

'Willie insisted on it,' said Jean bitterly. 'More than we ever did for our own bairns and cost us a fortune, it did.'

'Hush, woman.' And apologetically to the men: 'Photographs are an absolute essential for a potential thespian.'

'Thespian, indeed,' muttered Jean. 'She didn't take much of your advice, did she?'

Before this domestic argument swamped McGonagall's revelations, Faro interrupted: 'What about the unfortunate girl Polly's family?'

'She didn't talk much about them,' said Jean. 'They were tinker folk, attached to a travelling circus.'

'So you would find it very difficult to inform them.'

'Almost impossible, sir.' McGonagall sighed deeply. 'There are bands of these folk roaming the country, making camps outside towns. Sometimes they come to Magdalen Green, set up a penny gaff, a show under canvas, and by next morning they have vanished into thin air.'

'And mostly not empty-handed, either. They even steal clothes drying on the lines,' Jean put in. 'Kathleen always said Polly was ashamed of her background and wanted to better herself. You remember, Willie. She didn't like performing in a circus with wild animals, neither. Thought it wasn't ladylike. Said she smelt of lions all the time. Poor lass, oh, the poor lass.'

She began to cry again and this wakened the baby who added its dismal wail to the melancholy scene. As Jean rushed to the cradle, McGonagall jerked his head towards the door, a finger to his lips.

As they followed him into the corridor, Vince said comfortingly: 'No doubt Kathleen is still in London, but Polly changed her mind and came home.'

'Let us hope that was the way of it. I am feeling quite desperate, gentlemen.' He bit his underlip. 'I have a feeling that there is something – more than suicide in this.'

'What gave you that idea?' demanded Faro sharply.

'I detected a certain reluctance in the police officers to show me the body. And when at last they did, I was invited to sit down and answer a number of questions I would have considered quite unnecessary for the mere identification of a dead body.'

Pausing dramatically he surveyed his audience. 'Indeed I began to feel certain that – that, well, they suspected I had something to do with poor Polly's death. I became very indignant at such an idea.' And hanging his head, 'I am ashamed, quite ashamed, gentlemen, to admit to you that I vented my wrath on the unfortunate police constable who was questioning me before storming out in an attitude of high dudgeon.'

He leaned forward, put a finger to his lips and whispered: 'I am quite certain, gentlemen, that I was followed home.'

And springing forward, he twitched aside the curtain on the landing window. 'To be sure, I was right, gentlemen. Look for yourselves. He is still there. That is the very man standing at the corner.'

Faro looked down into the street and sighed. 'I'm afraid you're right.'

'So you do believe me, sir.' McGonagall seemed surprised.

'I believe you.'

Faro was in no danger of mistaking a police constable out of uniform, trying with difficulty and in extreme discomfort to look nonchalant and blend into the background.

McGonagall stared into Faro's face. 'You surely do not think they believe I have had something to do with that poor child's death?' There was unconcealed terror in his voice.

'Let us say I think they are just doing their duty. If you are the only person who has turned up to identify the body, then they are being ultra-cautious and getting as much information as they can.'

'But if I had committed this terrible crime, surely I wouldn't have gone near the police station? Surely my action proves my innocence,' McGonagall protested.

Faro shook his head. 'Not necessarily. There are those murderers who get their ultimate satisfaction in a final contemplation of their gruesome handiwork.'

McGonagall had paled visibly. 'Dear God, what am I to do?'

'Nothing. They'll give up after they get more evidence.'

'Evidence? You mean the invasion of my home, the terrifying of Mrs McGonagall? This is dreadful, sir, dreadful. It is bad enough having the worry of Kathleen without being involved in her friend's suicide.'

Faro was aware of a familiar prickling sensation in the region of his spine. The presence of the constable outside McGonagall's home confirmed that the police had reason to believe there was more to the girl's death than suicide.

Suicide was already the wrong word. Murder was more like it.

And there was only one way to find out.

Chapter Five

As they left Vince's lodging, Faro was unable to resist walking past the plain-clothes constable. 'Well done, lad. Keep it up,' he whispered.

The young man, recognising the voice of authority, saluted smartly thereby giving the whole game away. Faro raised an admonishing finger and with a sad shake of his head, still chuckling, caught up with Vince.

As they approached the town centre he asked idly where the police station was located.

'You are not going there, Stepfather? I thought you were on holiday?' There was no reply from Faro. 'You cannot resist a mystery, can you?'

'There is something wrong, Vince. Take my word for it.'

'Oh, for heaven's sake. That constable could have been watching the tenement. There's plenty of petty crime in Paton's Lane, believe me.'

When his stepfather remained silent, he said: 'Regarding the girl Polly, there is a perfectly logical explanation which I am sure must have occured to you almost immediately, as the reason for her suicide.'

'One you considered too indelicate to mention to McGonagall?'

Vince nodded grimly. 'Exactly. I suspect that neither of them went to London nor had they any intention of so doing. As you well know, in every big city, here and in Edinburgh, there are what are known in polite society as gentlemen's select clubs, patronised by the wealthy. And a positive refuge for young women whose ambitions are stronger than their morals.'

'Would Polly not have been more use to them alive than dead?'

'I think you'll get your answer from the police surgeon at the mortuary. I presume that is your destination,' he added in disgust.

When Faro mumbled: 'Something like that,' Vince continued: 'The answer is easy. The wretched girl probably found herself pregnant. In eight cases out of ten, that is the reason for suicides among young unmarried girls. Either betrayed and abandoned by a lover they cannot face the future or disowned by parents unwilling to endure a daughter's disgrace.'

Not either, sometimes both, thought Faro grimly, remembering how his dead wife Lizzie had been made to suffer, a fifteen-year-old servant girl, for bringing Vince into the world.

'Polly must have been pretty sharp about it,' he said, 'seeing that she had only gone missing for a few weeks.'

'Come, Stepfather, you can do better than that. I imagine that girls, the pretty ones with potential, are discovered and recruited on the weaving factory floor. Not literally, of course,' he added with a grin. 'They probably work part time in the select clubs until they soon find that working hours in both establishments and keeping up a pretence of home life are too exhausting and opt for the more lucrative nightwork. I would presume that Kathleen Neil wanted to spare McGonagall's feelings, hence the postcard from wherever it was posted.'

Faro was not convinced nor was he to be diverted from his purpose by Vince's argument.

He had no difficulty in identifying himself in the police station. They were fortunate, he was told, that the police surgeon had been called in to deal with a fatal accident enquiry. He was to be found in his temporary office.

'Is this an official enquiry?' asked Dr Ramsey nervously. He was young and clearly impressed to learn that

Dr Laurie had been assistant to the Edinburgh City police surgeon.

Vince quickly explained that his visit was on behalf of his landlady, Mrs McGonagall, quite distraught about a missing female relative. Ramsey listened with an expressionless face.

Then abruptly he led them to the mortuary and raised the sheet on a girl who had been pretty and voluptuous too. Surprisingly, however, the medical exchanges between Ramsey and Vince, including the fact that Polly Briggs had been a virgin, made nonsense of an unwanted pregnancy or indeed of prostitution.

Vince was also puzzled. 'I wonder why she committed suicide, then. An unhappy love affair, do you think?'

'Perhaps,' said Dr Ramsey.

'Have you any theories?' Faro asked.

'No. None at all. Now if you will excuse me, gentlemen . . . '

Faro looked sharply at the young doctor. His negative was a fraction too emphatic, his first eagerness to be helpful had faded rather suddenly. It indicated a refusal to discuss the subject any further, unusual between two doctors with a common background.

As they left that sad icy room of death they almost cannoned into a constable ushering a wild and distraught-looking man towards the door.

'Another poor soul come to identify a victim. God, how I used to hate those moments,' said Vince, 'when there is nothing you can say or do to give any comfort.'

At the front door, Faro paused. 'I think I will just pay my respects to Superintendent Johnston before I leave.'

Vince looked up at the clock. 'And I have a surgery in half an hour. See you later, Stepfather. Enjoy the play.'

'Are you not coming too?'

'Not tonight. I have an engagement.' With a gentle smile, 'Besides I've seen McGonagall's Macbeth twice already.'

48

'Oh. Is it worth my while?'

Vince laughed. 'Knowing your sensitivities, I wouldn't recommend it if I had any doubts. But this is a performance not to be missed. You have my word,' he added as they parted.

Faro was warmly welcomed by Superintendent Johnston, who had called upon his assistance on several occasions to investigate murder or fraud cases where there was involvement with an Edinburgh area.

'What brings you here?'

'My stepson, Dr Laurie, had business with Dr Ramsey. Concerning the girl who was found drowned. The suicide.'

The Superintendent nodded sympathetically. 'That was Briggs, her father, just gone along to make the formal identification. Poor man, he'd just heard about it. Someone read it in the paper and told him. Apparently the lass has been missing for weeks now. Tinkers they are, left their travelling circus in Fife. He's been searching for her everywhere.'

Faro looked up with new interest. 'I wonder, could I have a word with him before he leaves?'

At the Superintendent's puzzled glance, he said: 'My stepson lodges with the man McGonagall who came in earlier today. A young relative, a girl, was friendly with the dead lass. She is also missing.' His enquiring glance brought no response. Obviously the Superintendent knew nothing of any misfortune to Kathleen Neil.

'McGonagall, eh? We thought he might have done her in. Gave orders to have him watched. Looks weird and wild enough. But you can't go on appearances,' he added in what sounded like regret.

Promising to dine with the Superintendent and his wife on some future visit, Faro excused himself quickly and walked towards the mortuary where Polly's father was just emerging.

Overcome with grief, the tears spouting from his eyes, Briggs sobbed noisily into a large red handkerchief. To question him at such a time seemed a terrible intrusion into his agony.

'My condolences, sir,' said Faro. 'Come, let me help you to a seat – over here.'

'She's dead, my bonny bairn,' was the savage reply. 'What can you do to help?'

'I am a detective inspector, sir. We have knowledge that her friend Kathleen Neil with whom she lodged at the McGonagalls' was with her a few weeks ago. She is still missing. I am trying to trace her and any information you have might be of considerable assistance.'

'Kathleen Neil, that one. What's she done?'

'Nothing as far as I know. My enquiries are on behalf of her relatives who are naturally very concerned.'

'Oh I just wondered. Wouldn't put anything past that one. She was a thorough bad lot. If it hadn't been for her, our Polly would never have left home.'

'In what way did she influence your daughter?'

'They met when we were doing a penny gaff at Magdalen Green. We often called on members of the audience to do a turn and this Kathleen was persuaded by her uncle, or whoever he was, that actor chap, to do some bird calls.' And grudgingly, 'They were very good. She could have made a name for herself in the halls and seemed to have a liking for the travelling life. But she was ambitious and lazy and went back to the weaving after a day or two. Polly told us she had some well-off gent in tow who had promised to better her. We all know what that meant, of course,' he added scornfully.

'What happened then?' Faro ignored the implication.

'Our Polly just walked out on the circus. Went with her. Left home.' His sobs renewed. 'They'll never convince me that she took her own life. Oh dear God, dear God. That police doctor told me that she wasn't in the family way. As if any lass of ours would kill herself for that,' he said scornfully. 'There are no unwanted bairns with us. All are welcomed however they were come by. Welcomed, aye, and loved.'

'When did she leave home exactly?' asked Faro gently.

'About two months since, it would be. She had heard that there was money to be had in Dundee. The building of this bridge and so forth. There would be lots of chances for young lasses getting employment with Deane's.'

'And that was the last you heard of her?'

'Oh no. She came home a couple of times.'

'But there was no other communication?'

The man frowned. 'Communication?'

'I mean did she write at all?'

'We don't go much on writing, sir. Moving around all the time doesn't give much call for scholars. As long as we can count up the pennies that's all is needed. Last time we saw her was – I don't remember exactly – a few weeks ago.'

'That isn't very long. Did she perhaps go to London with her friend?'

'London? There was never any mention of London.' He made it sound like the ends of the earth. 'She was staying in Dundee and she promised faithfully to come home for her brother's wedding. When she didn't arrive we knew there was something wrong.'

'It might have been difficult for her getting back – if she did go to London.'

'London or Timbuctoo, what difference does it make? She would have come home for the wedding. A tinker lass's word is her bond. 'Sides she'd never have gone all that way to a foreign place without telling her family.'

Refusing Faro's offer of fare for a carriage back to Carnoustie, or for the train, as they neared Paton's Lane Briggs said proudly: 'Legs were made to walk on, sir. Mine have been carrying me on longer roads than that for fifty years now.'

Watching him walk away, their despondent farewell brought acute memories of that other bereaved father on the railway platform. And Faro remembered his promise to McGowan.

Could that have been only yesterday?

51

Retracing his steps to the police station, Faro asked the Sergeant in charge, Crail by name, if he might take at look at the accident log.

'Anything particular you're interested in, sir?' asked the Sergeant, torn between helpfulness and curiosity.

'A lad, Charlie McGowan, worked on the bridge.'

'Oh that one.' Flicking through the pages, he said: 'Here it is, sir.'

As Faro suspected, there was nothing in the entry to suggest it had been anything else but a platform that gave way on one of the piers. But turning over the pages for the last few months, he remarked:

'There do seem to be rather a lot of fatal accidents on the bridge.'

'What can you expect, sir? The Tay is notorious for high winds, it can pluck a body right off those pieces of iron, just as easy as winking,' Crail added with a kind of gruesome relish, and closing the logbook firmly: 'Anything else I can do for you, Inspector?'

Faro smiled. 'I'm curious to know why when I asked to see this particular entry you said: "Oh that one." '

The Sergeant raised his eyes heavenward. 'Oh, the poor laddie. We were all sorry about that, but his father just won't accept that it was an accident. According to him it was a personal vendetta between the lad and Deane's.' He touched his forehead significantly. 'Not quite right, you know. Grief gets them that way. We try to be sympathetic but what a trial he has been to us.'

'I understand his daughter-in-law, the lad's wife, also disappeared about the same time.'

Sergeant Crail gave a long-suffering sigh. 'Disappeared, left home. We put it on our missing persons list, of course, but when you've been on the force as long as I have, you know that if we stopped to investigate every case like that, we'd have no time left for crime. There's a dozen good reasons why a young widow should want to get away from it all and none of them very sinister.

52

'After all,' he added earnestly, 'perhaps she didn't care for her in-laws and we have only McGowan's word that she was happily married.'

Two missing women, two bereaved fathers mourning a son and a daughter, refusing to believe their deaths were accidental or self-inflicted but helpless to convince those in authority.

As for the girl Kathleen, he strongly suspected that she had never left Dundee either and all his instincts told him that Polly Briggs was a murder case. And that Dr Ramsey had his own reasons for silence.

He hated being baffled but any further investigations were the sole responsibility of Dundee City Police and as far as Detective Inspector Faro was concerned, the murderer's identity was of merely academic interest.

Too bad, but no doubt Vince would keep him informed of any interesting developments after his return to Edinburgh next week.

Chapter Six

Faro had the rest of the day to himself and was surprised to find that Dundee's rush of wealth had, perhaps as a result of Sir Arnold Deane's benevolence, proved a boon to the common man. As he wandered through Overgait and Nethergait he noted that the shops looked prosperous. Although their windows were less elegantly dressed than those of Edinburgh's Princes Street, their prices for the goods on display were considerably lower.

In the Wellgait he bought some twist tobacco for $3^1/_2$ pence per ounce, while wistfully eyeing Finest Old Highland Whisky at 16 shillings a gallon, Winter Claret at seven shillings and sixpence per dozen bottles and Invalid Port at 27 shillings per dozen quarts. Mrs Brook will be mortified to know how much more economically she could run our household, he thought, gleefully making a note of prices and handing over one shilling for a pound of her favourite tea to take back as a present.

His wardrobe, or lack of it, was a subject of constant reproach from both Vince and Mrs Brook, which he scornfully dismissed, pleading lack of time for such trivialities. Now in an unprecedented burst of extravagance he marched into a gentlemen's outfitters and purchased a handsome tweed suit, two shirts and two pairs of cotton drawers. Delighted to find that he still had change out of three pounds, he completed this wild spree at Paraphernalia's Shilling Store in the Overgait with a new tweed cap.

Made suddenly hungry by such reckless spending, he

tottered into the Old Steeple Dining Room and did full justice to an excellent three course meal of soup, steak and potatoes, and rice pudding for seven pence.

Only one penny less for an evening's entertainment at sixpence for a seat in the stalls at the Theatre Royal, he thought, studying the poster outside. With a boast of 'Accommodating audiences up to 1200 in number at each of its three performances nightly', it offered varied future attractions 'to suit the Entire Family.' From grand opera to prize-fighters, to 'Alpha Omega's Magic Circus, in which M Omega causes to vanish into thin air, tight-rope walkers, trapeze artists as well as performing poodles'.

Trudging back to Paton's Lane with his purchases as the shops were closing and gaslight flickered eerily across the piers of the now silent bridge, he found that Mrs McGonagall had lit a fire in his room.

Settling down to read before he went to the theatre, he took out the testimonials which McGonagall had pressed upon him.

'We willingly certify that the bearer, Mr William McGonagall, has considerable ability in recitation. We have heard him recite some passages from Shakespeare with great force; and are of the opinion that he is quite competent to read or recite passages from the poets and orators in villages and country towns with pleasure and profit to his audience. We also believe him to be a respectable man . . . '

And one signed by George Gilfillan, ending: 'he has a strong proclivity for the elocutionary department, a strong voice and great enthusiasm . . . '

Extraordinary, said Faro to himself, now almost eagerly anticipating the evening's entertainment as he struggled through the mass of people waiting to gain admission. He was heartily glad of his complimentary ticket.

Vince had been right. McGonagall's Macbeth was superb. Faro soon found himself transported beyond the shoddy set and threadbare costumes, the less than perfect performances of the supporting cast. He realised that this was in fact a one-man show and that McGonagall was quite capable of carrying the whole of Shakespeare's play single-handed.

With an audience who rose as one to give a standing ovation, Faro added his 'Bravo, bravo' to the calls and whistles and cheers as Macbeth staggered round the curtain. Sweat pouring from his forehead, McGonagall took his final bow.

As he walked back to Paton's Lane, Faro was still inspired, full of elation. Only one thing, he realised sadly, was missing to make the evening's enjoyment complete.

Even the world's best performance would have been bettered by the presence of a companion to share it with. If only Vince had been there. But at least the lad had seen it, they could discuss it together over a dram.

He was disappointed to find that the room was empty. Vince had not returned from his evening's engagement. The kitchen was occupied by a McGonagall daughter in charge of the sleeping infant.

No, her ma was out for the evening. So he was not even able to share his delight and congratulations with the actor's wife.

As he turned up the gas, the room, so threadbare and shabby, was dismal and cold too. His euphoria suddenly faded. There was something troubling him, at the back of his mind a shadow which threatened to loom large again.

This time it was something more personal and nearer home than the troubles of bereaved fathers and missing women. It was Vince. And as he tried to concentrate upon the newspaper he had brought in, his thoughts returned again to his stepson's new reticence.

In their Edinburgh days, Vince would normally have told him immediately what that 'previous engagement' was, especially as Faro had the strongest suspicion that it concerned Rachel Deane.

Such reticence was odd and disquieting, even if he had to accept the fact that he was now dealing with a new version of his stepson, a man in love, a character previously unknown to him and in many ways one who would increasingly become a stranger, secretive, withdrawn.

'Life is not lost which is spent or sacrificed in the grand enterprises of useful industry.'

He was staring at the notice of the fatal accident Vince had attended yesterday, a fifteen-year-old boy crushed to death by falling masonry. Angrily he thrust the newspaper away.

What infernal pomposity. How dare those who knew nothing of the suffering and endurance of the poor make such heartless wicked statements.

Turning for sympathy to Mr Charles Dickens who knew and understood such sentiments well, he began to read. After a few pages he realised he was not taking in one word. This shabby room was to blame, for his imagination was constantly imposing upon it the grandeur of Deane Hall.

Was that what was bothering him? Was his stepson in danger of making a totally unsuitable impossible marriage, a commitment to an heiress he could not hope to support?

Edwin Drood had no answer for him tonight and he sat down on the bed, took off his boots, undressed, washed in somewhat chilly water and got into bed. Grateful at least for Mrs McGonagall's warming pan, he turned away from the glare of lights from the bridge which touched his window and fell into an uneasy doze.

He was drifting off at last when the window rattled in a sudden gale. Cursing, he got out of bed, fixed a piece of newspaper to steady the frame and wearily settled down again, longing for the absolute silence of his bedroom in far-off Sheridan Place where all life was subdued from ten thirty onwards. There even the dawn chorus was a frowned-upon intrusion into the residents' privacy and early morning birds embarked upon their song with respectful harmony and timidity.

For seconds only it seemed he dozed once more, to be awakened by a nearby public house disgorging its customers in a roar of noisy goodnights.

Dundee, it seemed, never slept. The street below was in a furore of activity all night long. The new day had not yet lightened the sky when he was roused by the tramp of boots as men began their day's work on the bridge. Soon any further hopes of sleep were made impossible by the screech of cranes, the clang of rivets and the shouts of workmen calling to one another.

Tiptoeing into Vince's room, Faro contemplated the empty bed and realised that it was many years since he had lost sleep wondering where his stepson might be. But Vince and the imponderables of his love life were no longer the only source of Faro's anxiety.

The strange events of the last two days refused to be banished and a set of melancholy tableaux paraded themselves through his mind.

Always the detective, although the solving of these particular mysteries was no concern of his, he found himself making mental notes and now that there was sufficient daylight, he produced the writing materials he never travelled without. Wrapping himself in a blanket, he began to write in the hope that his observations and deductions might yield something to aid the Dundee detectives.

Half an hour later, his mind cleared, his hands frozen, he yawned and plumping up his pillow fell asleep, to be awakened by Vince vigorously shaking his shoulder.

'Wake up, Stepfather. Wake up.'

A pale gleam of sunshine penetrated the window curtain. Vince was saying cheerfully: 'Come along, Stepfather, breakfast is ready.'

Faro was too relieved to see his stepson in such good spirits to feel resentment at having been, as he put it later, 'dragged from sleep'. Shaved and dressed he found Vince

58

seated at Mrs McGonagall's table beside Willie who was giving his first performance of the day, reading a review from the *People's Journal*:

"'I have long been attracted to the acting of Mr William McGonagall and it was many years ago when he first attracted my attention. He had such a grim and ghastly look about him that I was impressed with the idea that he at least looked upon acting as a rather grave and important occupation." Ah, gentlemen, how right he was.

"'He had likewise such an air of sorrow and melancholy about him that one could not help thinking there was some cankering care or secret sorrow gnawing away his peace of mind. And yet if you watched him narrowly, you could observe that when any leading members got hissed for not playing their parts too well, a Mephistophelian gleam of pleasure would flit across his countenance which would afterwards change into a settled and self-conceited expression, as much as to say: 'If I only had the opportunity of playing those parts, I would soon show you how they should be acted!' " '

And throwing down the paper he beamed upon Faro and Vince. 'True, how true. And it all came to pass.'

He was delighted, puffed up with pride at Faro's very genuine pleasure in his Macbeth. To Faro's question as to how he became involved with Shakespeare's plays, he smiled.

'Even as a child the books I liked best were his penny plays, more especially *Macbeth*, *Richard III*, *Hamlet* and *Othello* and I gave myself no rest until I obtained complete mastery over these four characters. This I did, gentlemen, by grim determination in the evenings after fourteen hours at the weaving. Life was not easy then, we were very poor, always on the move. But even then, gentlemen, I knew I had a calling.'

Vince had to leave for a morning surgery and Faro accompanied him down the road. 'Did you have a good evening?' he asked, unable to restrain his curiosity any further when the information had not been volunteered.

'Not really, Stepfather. A bit of a disappointment. I decided to call upon Rachel, sure she would be at home in the evening and eager to receive me. I was told she had retired early with a headache.' A tone of exasperation and something worse. Anxiety, uncertainty, had crept into Vince's voice.

'I told that odious butler to kindly relay my message, but was informed he had orders that Miss Deane was not to be disturbed. Would I leave a message? I reminded him that I had already done so and would he impress upon his mistress that as my stepfather's time in Dundee is short, I would therefore present you to her this afternoon without fail.

'I was intending coming straight home, but I didn't like the look of one of the three fellows who were injured last week on the bridge. He is in the infirmary so I decided to pop round. There were, as I expected, complications and we had to do an emergency operation.'

'Will he recover?'

'I hope so. It really is intolerable, especially as I find all my protests about not having proper safety precautions are being ignored, set aside as too expensive. It seems to me sometimes that only men's lives are cheap.'

As they reached the crossroads Vince said: 'I'd better see how my patient is. What about you, Stepfather, how will you spend the morning?'

Assuring Vince that he could amuse himself until the visit to Rachel Deane, Faro decided to take the ferry across to Newport and have a closer look at the bridge from the other side of the river.

There was a strong wind blowing in from the sea and the groaning of the iron columns above his head did little to reassure him.

As a casual observer, unfamiliar with the world of engineering, he felt that nothing short of a miracle could ever safely bridge the spans of the two piers across that vast and turbulent expanse of water and gales.

It had all looked extremely perilous on a mild morning

when he had parted from Vince. Since then the day had deteriorated rapidly. Heavy clouds scurried across the sky making for a blustery stroll and he had to be content with a very brisk walk facing into an unpleasantly fierce wind whipping the river into a white foam.

As he feared, his return journey across the two-mile stretch of water was accompanied by all the less engaging qualities of open sea as far as his stomach was concerned.

Far above his head, creaking cranes and pulleys elevated baskets of enormous dimensions up the piers, presumably containing building materials. This activity was accompanied by warning shouts and directions from the workmen who bravely crouched on frail platforms where wooden screens served as shields to protect them from vagaries of wind and weather. On the sandbanks the seals, which Vince had told him to look out for, had wisely disappeared.

The rain began as he stepped ashore and decided him to indulge in a more luxurious meal than could be found in the Old Steeple Dining Hall. In the Glamis Hotel, encouraged by a handsome fire and sofas waiting invitingly in the main reception room, he was able to ignore the gloomy prospect outdoors.

Summoned to the dining room, he had just taken two spoonfuls of excellent Scotch broth when the walls reverberated to the sound of gunfire. The other diners promptly left their places and surged to the windows.

'What on earth is going on?' he demanded. 'Have we been invaded?'

Had something disastrous overtaken that Auld Alliance between France and Scotland in the short while he had been absent from Edinburgh? And staring over the diners' shoulders, he wondered if war had broken out although there had been no alert at the Central Office from England's network of spies.

'-four-five-six-seven-'

He was aware of the diners chanting at each explosion.

'Eight. Eight!'

The magic word was greeted by a cheer and a hurrah.

Seeing his solemn face one of the waiters said: 'Eight of them! Isn't that marvellous?'

'Eight of what?'

'Why sir, eight whales of course. That's the *Excelsior* – one of the whaling fleet just returned. The gunfire is the signal of how many whales they've caught.'

'Oh, is that all?' said Faro returning to his soup. What an extraordinary place this was.

'Frightened me out of my wits. Can you imagine anyone in Edinburgh getting excited if a whaling ship came up the Forth?' he said to Vince when they met in readiness for the visit to Deane Hall, by which time the shoreline was already crowded with an enthusiastic group of townsfolk.

Vince smiled. 'You get used to it. Although I'd better warn you there'll be no sleep for anyone tonight. The inns will be packed, doing a thriving business. All the ladies of the town will be out in full force. I understand they come by boat from all up and down the east coast when the fleet is expected.'

Vince paused and then added, 'Talking of whalers, I've been thinking about McGonagall's girl. Perhaps she went off with the fleet, they do occasionally take their fancy women aboard. Although it's supposed to be forbidden, the authorities are pleased to turn a blind eye.'

'Well, we should soon see whether your theory is correct, Vince. If she walks into the house in the next day or two. I shall look to you to keep me informed about the missing Kathleen as well as any other developments in the case.'

Vince laughed. 'My dear Stepfather, don't look so doleful.'

'Doleful?'

'Yes, you really are addicted to crime, aren't you?'

'Perhaps so, but I shall have to restrain myself this time, since this is out of my territory.'

'And do I detect that you wish it wasn't?' When Faro

shrugged, Vince continued cheerfully: 'Never mind, you will be back in Dundee very soon, remember. And your next visit will be a happy and memorable one. For our wedding. There's a family chapel in the grounds and that's where Rachel wants the ceremony to take place. Since you are not my real father, I would like you to be best man.'

'I would be delighted, lad. But surely there is some friend of your own age?'

Vince shook his head firmly. 'No one I would rather have than my very best friend – and stepfather.'

Touched and flattered, Faro asked: 'Have you fixed a date?'

'Rachel wants it as soon as she comes of age officially. It's incredibly near now, just a few weeks away.'

'No regrets or second thoughts, eh?'

'Not a single one, Stepfather. I am the happiest man in the whole world. Every day we are apart I find hard to bear. I want to be with her every moment. After our precious days and nights together, it is agonising that we should have to live apart again.'

The carriage swung round in the direction of Deane Hall. 'Especially with Rachel living away up here and me down in Paton's Lane,' he added. 'After all, we consider ourselves man and wife for we have exchanged the only vows that really matter.'

Looking out of the window, smiling shyly, he said softly: 'We are married, Stepfather, in every way but the legal formalities.'

As the carriage approached the lodge gates with their stone griffons Faro would have given a great deal to share in his stepson's happy confidence in a future that seemed to him fraught with problems.

The door opened promptly and the butler deigned to bow. 'Dr Laurie, sir. Mr Faro. Please come in. Miss Deane is expecting you.' Across the hall, he led the way to a handsome set of double doors. 'Would you please wait in the library while I announce you.'

63

Left alone with Vince, Faro whistled. 'What a room, what a place to sit and read in.' He did not number among his vices, envy of other men's possessions. But these extravagant surroundings fulfilled the requirements of his wildest dreams, his hopeless ambition to possess a well-stocked library.

Each wall was stacked from floor to ceiling with oak bookshelves containing behind their glass doors a collection of handsome leather-bound volumes. A log fire blazed cheerily in a stone fireplace and two steps led up to a magnificent bow window whose padded seat overlooked a sloping garden. Beyond were spread out the hills of Forfarshire.

Faro had little time to do more than glance at the book titles and discover that most were first editions and many signed by the authors. As he sighed over a volume of *Heart of Midlothian* by Sir Walter Scott – 'To Arnold Deane with the author's compliments' – footsteps on the hall's marble floor announced the returning butler.

'Miss Deane will see you now, gentlemen.'

They followed him through the richly carpeted hall where two wings of an intricately carved oak staircase climbed graciously upwards beneath a handsome stained-glass window depicting Scotland's heroes, William Wallace and Robert the Bruce, flourishing broadswords.

At their approach two maids and a footman melted discreetly into the woodwork and Faro whispered to Vince: 'One would think we were royalty.' Privately he thought that the highly publicised manners and customs of their dear Queen had much to answer for. This new and affluent upper middle class had shown great alacrity in adopting such snobberies.

The butler opened double doors into a drawing room which was the size of a ballroom, a function Vince later told him it had fulfilled on many great occasions in the past before Sir Arnold's illness. And of course, it would do so again. When Rachel and he were married, this was to be the magnificent setting for their wedding reception.

Faro guessed as they walked across the floor that this room must cover the entire first floor level of the house. Windows faced south and west, dazzling crystal chandeliers tinkled above their heads, heavy Aubusson carpets cushioned their feet.

A huge fireplace well-stocked with logs promised warmth to a girl who was dwarfed by the depths of the Carolean armchair and by the splendour of her surroundings.

She was smaller than Faro had imagined, her dark hair coiled on top of her head. And in the short time they were to be in her presence, Faro realised a deep sense of disappointment, and of revelation.

He had naturally expected that Vince would have chosen a beauty for his wife. His selection of young Edinburgh ladies had always indicated a preference for the loveliest of girls and only once, when he had been briefly infatuated with an older women, the police surgeon's wife, had this preference faltered.

But this girl, who was to be his ultimate choice, was none of these. True, her hair was raven black and her eyes might well be violet but a screen behind the chair, presumably to keep her from draughts, also excluded any sun from the windows, sufficiently dimming the vast room's remaining light which might have served to accentuate her charms.

He looked quickly at Vince whose face was radiant with adoration. Well, well, beauty was indeed in the eye of the beholder, since his stepson's description had led him to expect a Helen of Troy or a Cleopatra, goddess extraordinary instead of mere girl ordinary in the extreme. To his untutored eye, she appeared rather plain.

In the brief moments before she spoke, Faro, who was used to making rapid assessments of personalities since much of his work and often his life depended on swift judgements, decided that she must have some unknown qualities apparent only to a lover, that transformed her into an irresistible paragon of sparkle and animation.

I must not be so uncharitable, so ungallant, he told himself sternly. I should be delighted, gratified, since it appears that Vince has taken to heart my advice that there was more to love and a life partner than a pretty face.

But his initial disappointment was soon quenched by more important factors.

As Vince went forward to greet his beloved, Faro had remained at a discreet distance, easy to achieve in that vast room. He stared out of the window, admiring the view and allowing the lovers a little time to themselves.

The girl's voice alerted him and turning he witnessed something stranger than the scene of sweet dalliance he had expected.

'I beg you to say no more, Dr Laurie. I can only presume that the urgency of your wish to see me concerns my grandfather's health. Pray be seated.'

Although the girl spoke softly her voice reached with a bell-like clarity to where he hovered waiting to be invited forward.

The words were either a joke or a bombshell. Faro looked across at Vince, who remained smiling tenderly down at the girl. A joke obviously, he thought with relief. A little game for lovers. She was pretending, teasing him. Well, well, was that the secret of her allure?

Still smiling, Faro moved nearer. But his presence had been forgotten.

Vince was no longer smiling. 'Rachel – dearest – for heaven's sake. What is all this about?'

Rachel Deane looked beyond Vince and saw Faro. 'Sir,' the appeal was directed at him. 'I received you both because Dr Laurie is my grandfather's physician. Indeed Sir Arnold thinks very highly of him. But when he knows how his trusted doctor has abused his rôle to press his unwelcome attentions in this manner – and invade my privacy, I think he may come to change his mind.'

Faro looked from one to the other in bewilderment. If this was a joke being staged for his benefit, then it was being played too hard and had gone too far for his taste.

He watched Vince spring forward and in an agitated manner attempt to seize Rachel's hands. He watched him sink on to his knees before her, saw her wrench her hands away, cowering far back in her chair.

'Sir – Mr Faro – please – be so kind as to remove this – this gentleman from my presence. Or must I call the servants.'

Faro went forward, put a restraining hand on Vince's arm. He noticed how it trembled.

'Vince, lad, what on earth has happened?' he whispered.

'I will answer that, sir,' said Rachel. 'This – this creature with whom you seem to have some acquaintance and influence, claims that I – that I am his betrothed, that we are to marry soon. This is preposterous, ridiculous. You have my word, sir, that although I have heard his name mentioned by my grandfather, I have never set eyes on him before in my whole life.'

Chapter Seven

'Rachel, for God's sake. Is this some kind of joke? You know perfectly well that it was through Sir Arnold that we first met. Oh my dearest girl, you can't have forgotten that. You can't have forgotten Errol –' his voice dropped to a whisper – 'the cottage where we stayed together.'

'The what? Are you mad? I never set foot in any cottage with you. Sir!' Again she appealed to Faro. 'You look respectable enough – can you not restrain this creature?'

'For God's sake, Rachel. Don't pretend not to have heard of him either. He is my stepfather, Detective Inspector Faro of Edinburgh City Police.'

Her eyes widened. The information seemed to take her by surprise, as indeed it must if she had never met Vince Laurie before.

'Then I presume you can vouch for this gentleman.'

Argument was futile. 'I can indeed, Miss Deane.'

She shrugged. 'At least I am not being confronted by a madman, for that was my first impression. But now I can see that he has been the victim of some wicked practical joke.'

'A joke you say. Is that all you can call it? All our – our days – our nights together.' Again Vince knelt before her, tried to seize her hands and was pushed away.

'Dearest girl, tell me the truth. Are the family forcing you to deny me, to deny that we are lovers? Is that what's the matter? Is it, is that all it is, my darling?'

Leaning forward he attempted to embrace her, but she

68

half rose from her chair and seizing the bellpull tugged at
it. The sound reverberated and the door opened with such
alacrity that Faro could only conclude that the butler had
been posted to listen outside.

'Please show these gentlemen out, Robson.'

'Yes, Miss Deane.'

'But Rachel – you can't – you can't do this to me.'

The butler had a firm grip on Vince's arm. It almost
suggested that at one time he might have served with the
police too. 'Come along, sir,' he said in the manner of
one humouring a madman.

As Vince struggled, Robson gave Faro a helpless look.
There was nothing he could do but bow briefly to Rachel
Deane and follow his stepson from the room with as much
dignity as was left to him.

At the foot of the stairs there was a short scuffle as
Vince, recovering from that initial shock, made a valiant
attempt to race back upstairs and confront Rachel. This
time Faro showed no hesitation. He assisted the butler.

'Come along, lad.'

'But – but –' Bewildered, Vince was close to tears.

'There, there, lad.' The door opened rapidly, closed
just as swiftly behind them. 'There, there. We'll think
of something. Don't you worry.'

The Glamis Hotel was nearer than Paton's Lane, its
surroundings soothing and impersonal, preferable to the
bleak depressing bedroom and the risk of an encounter
with the McGonagalls.

Faro thrust Vince up the steps. 'We wish to be private.
Have you a room?' he asked at the desk.

'Across there, sir. We use it for private functions.'

'Excellent.' Following the bellboy, Faro propelled
Vince into the room with its plush sofas and long
table. The young man sat down meekly, still too dazed
and numb for protest.

Faro ordered a bottle of whisky, much to the waiter's
surprise. He clearly wasn't used to such generous orders.

'And two glasses.'

The waiter brought the order, his manner cautious and apprehensive as he stared at Vince, clearly wondering what these two gentlemen were up to. Were they in disagreement? Faro could see him nervously moving glasses and considering what was breakable in the room, as if anticipating an imminent bout of fisticuffs.

In any other circumstances he would have found it entertaining. And so would Vince. But neither had much heart left for amusement.

Faro poured out a generous measure. 'Drink it, lad. Go on. You'll feel better.'

Vince barely raised his head. 'Better? I never felt so vile in my whole life. I wish I was dead. She loves me. She is my wife – my wife, you understand. We have been lovers. And now – to deny it completely. To deny even knowing me. Oh dear God, what has come over her? She cannot be so cruel.'

He thumped his fist upon the table. 'What am I to do, Stepfather? How can I win her back? Tell me what to do, for God's sake – before I go mad.'

So saying he crashed down the whisky glass and began pacing back and forth to the window as if expecting some miracle in the shape of Rachel Deane to appear, his actions carefully watched by the nervous waiter who hovered by the private bar.

'Sit down, Vince. Sit down,' said Faro. 'I can do nothing to help you until we calmly consider all that has happened.'

'Calmly – how can I consider my broken heart, her cruel treatment calmly?'

'Because that is the way you have been taught to think, lad. It is the way you were reared, the way you have lived all your life with me,' said Faro sternly. 'If you are speaking truth – and I don't doubt that for a moment, then Miss Deane is lying. And if she is lying, then there has to be some reason. And we must find it.'

'She wouldn't lie. She is good and true—'

'Vince, listen to me. There is a mystery here and it has to be solved like any other mystery. And the sooner you calm yourself, the sooner we will find our answer.' Replenishing the glasses, he said: 'First of all, I want the evidence.'

'Evidence?'

'Indeed. I want you to tell me the whole story of your meeting with Miss Deane and what led to your further association. Rest assured I shall neither condemn nor condone but I beg you, leave nothing out.'

'It all began one day', said Vince, 'when Sir Arnold was visiting the factory. Before his illness he came at regular intervals to inspect the working conditions and showed a lively interest in the workers. If a man or a woman had problems, he was never too grand to sit down and discuss their difficulties with them. He was, and is, greatly loved, a fine man.

'One morning during his perambulations he collapsed. Fortunately I happened to be on hand, since my surgery and my patients' records were something he might wish to inspect. He made a note of all details of accidents and in the case of deaths would write a personal note, with a few guineas, to the dependants.

'I could see at once that he had suffered a mild stroke. I took the necessary steps to revive him and he was grateful, insisted I had saved his life and asked that I should continue to attend him, as his personal physician was an old man who, Sir Arnold said, should have retired years ago.

' "I like having young men with young ideas around me."

'We got along famously and it was on one of my weekly visits to Deane Hall that I first met Rachel. As I was leaving she rushed downstairs to the hall and thanked me for all I had done for her grandfather. On my next visit I found I had to attend her as a patient. She had slipped on the stair and sprained her ankle. It wasn't serious but I think it was at that moment we

71

looked into each other's eyes and we both knew what was happening.

'I know what follows sounds like madness, Stepfather, but you must be patient with me. She began visiting the factory, allegedly bringing clothes for some of the poorer workers, but she always did so when I was at my surgery. One day as she was leaving I took her in my arms and the next moment we were confessing our undying love for each other. I think I even asked her to marry me, although I hardly expected that a humble factory doctor would be seriously considered as a prospective suitor.

'On her next visit, she told me that she would be honoured and indeed proud to be my wife, but we must wait until she came of age, then she could do as she pleased. She told me that she longed for me, that such waiting time was intolerable and she had arranged with a friend, an old nurse, that we should visit her cottage for a few days. Did I think that a good idea?

'Of course I did. I was deliriously happy at the prospect. We arranged to meet on Magdalen Green.'

He looked at Faro appealingly. 'Even then, I thought I was dreaming. I could hardly believe that she would be there, that it was true. But she arrived promptly in a carriage which she said was engaged to carry us to Dundee Railway Station. Errol she said was our destination—'

'Errol, did you say?' Faro interrupted. And when Vince gave him a questioning glance, he said: 'No – pray continue.'

'After purchasing our tickets, we sat in the train like two happy children playing truant. It was a short walk from the station before we turned through lodge gates into a vast estate where Rachel said her nurse's cottage was situated.

'I was a little taken aback, but enormously gratified, to find that there was no sign of any servants, or of the old nurse, who I had imagined would look after us and probably prove to be a stern chaperone. I had not the least idea then that Rachel intended to anticipate our marriage, that we were to become lovers.

'She had thought of everything. Before we met that day she had been into the Overgait and had purchased a picnic hamper, filled it with provisions, bread, wine, chicken, ham, a Dundee cake, enough for several days. We would certainly not go hungry and so we feasted, avoiding any of the estate workers as we walked in the vast woods. The house itself when we were near enough to inspect it, was shuttered. The family, she said, went to Italy each spring.

'At last it was over, we had run out of time. Time I had begged off from my surgery with the excuse of an urgent visit to Edinburgh. Time she had stolen to visit a sick friend in Perth.

'On the last day, almost tearfully we walked back to the station and took the train back to Dundee. I saw her into a carriage bound for Deane Hall and returned lonely and desolate, but full of hope for the future, to Paton's Lane. That night I wrote to tell you of my good fortune. But that is the last time I saw Rachel until our meeting with her this afternoon.'

Faro was deeply concerned with his stepson's story. The lad was too well balanced to have imagined the events of the last two weeks. He was not even romantic by temperament and had enjoyed great successes with the ladies until now without being under any obligation. Experienced where women were concerned, he was not of that nature who might in desperation mistake flirtation for serious intent.

Strongest of the evidence in Vince's favour was his natural antipathy towards the matrimonial state. It was Rachel's behaviour that was completely baffling. Why should a well brought up young girl in a strata of society which made the strictest demands of morality suddenly throw convention aside and elope with a young man she hardly knew?

'Did you have any reason to suspect her behaviour was at all – well, odd?'

73

'I am not sure what you mean.'

'Did she tell you anything in those few days about her background, her life as a child?'

Vince smiled into the middle distance. 'Only that she was often naughty. She hated being told what to do and – and—' He paused frowning.

'Well?'

'I remember recalling that her grandfather once told me that although he loved her dearly, she was his only grandchild, she was often wilful and naughty. A wild child, subject – subject to erratic fits. She would be over the moon as he put it, one minute, and the next sunk into deepest melancholy.'

Vince was silent now, looking at him as if there should be some ready answer. 'I wonder now could such fits be drug-induced, brought about by taking laudanum? As you probably know, Stepfather, lots of young girls take it for menstrual disorders and her grandfather once asked me to prescribe it for her, for exactly that condition.'

'Without you seeing the patient, Vince? Surely that is irregular?'

'I suppose it was. And had it been anyone else but Sir Arnold I would have refused. She did talk to me about this problem when we were in Errol, of course, so it was quite genuine.'

It was Faro's turn to be silent. 'Was there anyone who might have seen you together?'

'Only the guard at the station. I doubt whether he would remember us though. He hardly looked up when we handed in our tickets.'

'Estate workers then?'

'Well, we tried to avoid them wherever possible. After all, we were trying to be discreet. We weren't exactly eager to brazenly announce to the world that we were anticipating our marriage vows.'

And that fact didn't make sense either, thought Faro. What was all the hurry? Why didn't Rachel wait a few

74

weeks until she came of age and could please herself in the choice of a husband?

In the few minutes he had been in her company he would have said that her reactions were exactly what he would have expected of the heiress of Deane. She certainly did not strike him as a lass who would throw her bonnet over the windmill and indulge in a passionate premarital love affair.

'Tell me something about this estate. Was there anything special that you could recognise again?'

'Of course I could find it. I have a map that Rachel brought with her. I carry it still,' he said softly, 'as a memento.' Producing it from his pocket book he spread it before Faro. 'See, there, the area ringed. That's where we stayed. It's just off the main road to Perth, at the signpost for Errol.'

Faro had a sudden feeling of triumph. 'Did it have twin lodges with tiny turrets and two spread eagles on the gateposts?'

Vince gasped. 'Exactly that. But how did you know?'

'Because, my dear lad, there is only one estate at Errol large enough to answer that description. And what is more, my friend Tom Elgin is gamekeeper on the adjoining estate.' He rubbed his hands gleefully. 'This is marvellous. Why, I stayed with him the night after Will Gray's funeral.'

'And you still remember the twin lodges?' said Vince in amazement. 'In your befuddled condition?'

'Old habits die hard, lad. Observation is second nature, and often an absolute necessity for my survival. And this time it is going to be invaluable, to prove that you were telling the truth.'

'You mean—' Hope flooded Vince's pale face.

'I mean that I shall visit Tom and see that cottage and the nurse.'

'The nurse, of course. She'll tell you that Rachel contacted her.'

Vince's mood swiftly changed from gloom to optimism.

75

For the moment, the account of his love affair had been in the nature of an expurgation. To his stepfather's suggestion that he might now wish to return to his lodgings, he said firmly:

'What on earth for? I'll only sit and brood and I've done enough of that for one day. Rachel may have spurned me for her own good reasons, but meantime there are other people who need me.' And consulting the wall clock, 'I have a surgery at the factory at five. Yes, I will be perfectly all right and I'll see you later this evening, I hope. Perhaps by that time you will have some evidence that will make Rachel admit that she loves me. It will make a change for you, this solving an affair of the heart, instead of a crime,' he added cynically.

Faro merely smiled. But he left wondering what was to be gained from the proposed visit, beyond the satisfaction of proving that Vince and Rachel had indeed visited Errol. And would it do the lad any good to learn that his beloved was a heartless liar?

As for solving enigmas of behaviour, whether criminal or in the human heart, there seemed little difference really. The puzzle lay deep in the labyrinth of personality, full of twists and turns and unsolved clues which German psychologists were only beginning to unravel.

Chapter Eight

At Paton's Lane Jean McGonagall was industriously scrubbing the front step.

'Oh, it's yourself, Inspector. I was just telling Willie, when I first saw you I thought you must be Dr Laurie's elder brother,' she added with a shy giggle. 'You look far too young to be his father.'

'His stepfather, actually,' he reminded her.

'Oh, is that it?' she answered vaguely as if she was still considering that possibility and would have liked to question him further. As he walked towards the stairs he thanked her for putting a warming pan in his bed and leaving warm water. Even if it was cold by the time he used it he realised it had to be got from a pump in the yard, carried up several flights of stairs and heated.

'I hope you are comfortable with us, sir,' she said anxiously. 'We haven't much as you know. We're that upset about poor Polly Briggs. Fancy doing herself in, the poor lassie. What on earth came over her to do a thing like that?' And with a sad shake of her head. 'I just canna take it in somehow.'

Her eyes filled with tears and she paused to wipe them on her apron. 'I expect our Kathleen will come for the funeral. Like sisters they were. I canna think that she would stay away.'

And Faro, listening, thought grimly, only if she too is dead. Out loud he said: 'Maybe she doesn't know, Mrs McGonagall. I mean, if she's in London, such news might not reach her.'

'Maybe so, maybe so. I'm right worried, sick with worry I am. I don't know where to turn.' And studying Faro's face hesitantly, 'Do you think you could help us? We were wondering if you might know someone in the police who could tell us how to go about finding our Kathleen?'

Faro refrained from replying that he and the Dundee City Police put together lacked the ability to work miracles. 'I will do anything I can, of course, but trying to find a missing person in London would be like searching for the proverbial needle—'

'In the proverbial haystack, sir.' The door behind them had opened and William McGonagall appeared. 'I've told you not to fuss, woman. Kathleen will turn up when she has a mind to do so. And now do go about your business, woman, and stop pestering Inspector Faro with our worries.'

As Jean went into the kitchen he said: 'A word in your ear, sir. About the girl. I am certain that she has found employment nearer home than London.' He winked at Faro nudging his arm. 'Delicacy forbids me mentioning the matter before Mrs McG. Women worry about their ewe lambs, but fathers like ourselves, we are men of the world. God gave us a deeper understanding.'

He glanced quickly heavenward as if expecting divine approval. 'For instance, there is the whaling fleet. A custom not freely known among respectable womenkind like my dear spouse, but the men do sometimes take lasses away on voyages with them. Lasses who are not their wives, if you get my drift.'

So Vince had informed him.

'Ah yes, sir, to be a man of the world is neither to condemn nor to condone,' McGonagall continued, 'a quality beautiful to behold among those of us who are thespians. We know the lure of the footlights. Kathleen was always stage-struck, with her bird calls and all. She envied Polly that travelling circus the tinkers lived with. She lacked a certain interest in the Bard,' he added with a regretful pursing of his lips, 'but with a little encouragement and training I could make her a great tragedienne—'

'Which reminds me,' Faro interrupted, 'that I have not thanked you for my ticket last night. I was enthralled by your performance.'

'Enthralled,' William repeated delightedly. 'You were enthralled. Alas, it was far from my best performance. The shock I had sustained earlier that day and so forth—'

'Mr McGonagall, take it from me, your Macbeth was brilliant.' Faro exclaimed. 'I have never seen better. You can take my word for it. Even on the Edinburgh stage, and we get the London actors like Kean and Irving each year.'

'Is that true?' McGonagall beamed. 'Sir Edmund and Sir Henry. Well, well, sir, that is the greatest compliment you could pay me. I am most grateful to you, for an actor succeeding in living out a rôle is beautiful to be seen. I understand from Dr Laurie that you are also a worshipper at the shrine of the Swan of Avon. "To be, or not to be: that is the question: Whether 'tis nobler in the mind—" '

' "—to suffer The slings and arrows of outrageous fortune, Or to take arms against a sea of troubles, And by opposing end them?" '

McGonagall applauded, vigorously nodding approval and Faro hid a smile. He was being tested and McGonagall studied him keenly, thrusting out his lower lip.

'Indeed, sir, had you not chosen a life of criminology we might have made a tragedian out of you.' Standing back he looked him up and down. 'You have a fine imposing figure, an excellent profile and you belong as do us thespians to that category of men who carry their years lightly and grow better with maturity. By the time you are forty you will not yet be in your prime and at the age when an actor's voice has just reached its best.'

79

'I am forty and more,' smiled Faro.

'Then you are very fortunate, for you have worn extremely well.' Narrowing his eyes, McGonagall said, 'You have the tall Viking look. I can see you as one of the great Nordic heroes, even a Siegfried.'

Faro laughed. 'You know, I think I would prefer being a policeman. I don't think I was cut out for heroics.'

'Only off-stage, is that it, Inspector?' McGonagall laughed. 'You are too modest I fear. Let it be, let it be. You are not yet too old for the profession should you change your mind. We need mature actors for the Bard's great rôles, for Othello and Lear.'

When Faro repeated the conversation to Vince later, his stepson exploded into mirth. 'That caps all, Stepfather, really it does. You – an actor—'

Since McGonagall's claims, although far-fetched, had also been extremely flattering, as Vince doubled up with laughter, Faro said in injured tones: 'I don't think it was all that amusing.'

'I had a sudden vision of you in black face as Othello. I wish you could have seen it. Priceless, priceless.'

Faro felt his moment of hurt pride was well worth it, to see Vince able to laugh again. He had feared that with Rachel Deane's rejection something young and boylike might have been snuffed out for ever. Now he felt oddly optimistic as he considered what possible reasons lurked behind her denial of her own true love and of the idyll they had shared. And of what strange truths he might uncover during that visit to Errol.

And staring out of the train window as it headed towards Perth, Faro wished that he was at liberty to investigate Polly Briggs' 'suicide', Charlie McGowan's accident, the riddle of the two missing women, and to discover whether there was any connecting link.

Deciding that such a coincidence was playing one of his famous intuitions too far, with a sigh he realised that he must content himself with trying to solve the less dangerous but nonetheless intriguing mystery which was so important to his stepson: the enigma of Rachel Deane's extraordinary behaviour.

As Errol drew nearer his mood of optimism evaporated. Even if this visit proved that Vince spoke the truth, what difference could it make to his cause? Again he realised that proof of the cottage's existence could not force Rachel to admit that she had lied if she had deliberately hardened her heart to her former lover.

Faro had built up a mental picture of a girl who was subject to strange moods, to prolonged fits of melancholy. While Vince had accepted the medical theory, the full significance of her condition and its bearing on any permanent relationship between them seemed to have escaped him.

Faro's own conclusions were that Rachel had formed an infatuation for Vince and had embarked on an amorous adventure with him. When she returned to Deane Hall from their short idyll, she had either regretted her impulse or had been persuaded by her family that she was about to embark upon an unfortunate or even an impossible marriage.

Faro could sympathise with Rachel's family. Indeed he would have been the first to agree heartily. Even from his less involved point of view, it was obvious that a poor doctor was no suitable husband for an heiress.

But surely the girl could have been persuaded to choose a less cruel and heartless way of rejecting him?

The lodge gates were still there as he remembered them and as he walked down the drive towards the gamekeeper's cottage, he was relieved to see Tom Elgin returning with his gun under his arm.

His friend was surprised and delighted to see Jeremy Faro again especially as, at Will Gray's funeral, both had deplored that only on such melancholy occasions did they ever meet these days.

'You're the last person I expected to see. Don't tell me there's another funeral in the offing.'

Faro laughed. 'Not at all. As you know, I'm staying in Dundee and as my stepson is busy all day doctoring, I decided to take you up on your offer.'

As he took a seat at the fireside, Faro realised again that this typical estate cottage was similar to the one that Vince had described. Two panelled rooms downstairs, with a narrow staircase leading to two bedrooms with sloping ceilings and dormer windows.

Taking the whisky bottle from the cupboard, Tom Elgin poured out a couple of generous drams. 'Slàinte!'

Lighting a pipe, he regarded his friend through the smoke. 'Well, well, Jeremy, so what brings you here, besides another crack with an old crony?'

Faro laughed. 'What makes you think I have a purpose in mind?'

Tom gave him a shrewd glance. 'Once a policeman, always a policeman. As soon as I saw you walking down the drive, scrutinising everything very carefully, I guessed that this was more than a social visit, pleasant though that would be.'

As Faro hesitated, Tom asked: 'Don't tell me the laird has been misbehaving himself?'

'Not at all, at least, not that I know of. No, this is a personal matter and in strictest confidence.' And Faro plunged into the extraordinary story of Vince's love affair and its disastrous ending.

'How astonishing that the young woman should have denied it all. Even that they had ever met.' And frowning, Tom asked the inevitable question.

Faro had his answer ready. 'No, old friend, there is not the remotest possibility that Vince was not speaking the truth. I trust his word absolutely. I was there too, when she denied it.'

And without revealing Rachel's identity, he described Deane Hall and the way she had received them.

When he had finished, Tom looked thoughtful. 'There

is another reason, of course, that has doubtless occurred to you. The lass may have been under considerable pressure from her own family. This grand room, what was it like?'

'The size of a ballroom.'

'Ah,' said Tom significantly. 'Could her parents have been listening somewhere nearby, out of sight? Just to make sure she was speaking as she had been instructed.'

Faro looked up quickly. Taken aback by Rachel's denial he had allowed bafflement and concern over Vince's violent reaction to blind him to the obvious.

'Once a policeman, always a policeman, as you said, Tom. And by God, I think you have something there, something I never even considered. The drawing room was huge and more dimly lit than was comfortable. There were plenty of chandeliers, so it did strike me that they were being rather frugal.'

As he remembered that scene he thumped his fists together. 'Dammit, there was even a large screen behind the armchair.'

Tom gave a nod of satisfaction. 'And I would wager, someone behind it too. Listening to every word.'

Faro shook his head sadly. For once his own much vaunted powers of observation had failed him. Undeniable proof that even experienced, well-trained detectives are capable of not recognising what is staring them in the face.

Eagerly he seized upon this idea of Rachel Deane being coerced by her family. Tom had given him new hope.

'Rachel – did you say that was the girl's name?'

'Yes.' It had slipped out, but never mind.

'Could that be Rachel Deane?'

'The same. You know her?'

'Only vaguely. I wouldn't recognise her now, but I knew her when she was a wee lass.' Tom whistled. 'The Deane heiress. Well, well, now I'm not altogether surprised at what you've told me.'

'Indeed?'

83

'Yes. I've heard tales of her odd behaviour before. A constant stream of governesses. Went through them like pounds of bannocks, according to her old nurse.'

'You knew her nurse?'

'Not knew – know her. Amy is still very much alive and kicking.' With a shake of his head, he added, 'And the way Amy tells it, she was the only one who could do anything with Miss Rachel. Her mother was a Balfray, you know, and their estate bordered on this one, the other end of the wood. I'll take you across if you like. Dougie, the factor, is an old crony of mine.'

As they climbed the stile, Faro had a sudden feeling of triumph. There was Vince's cottage with its apple tree, the tiny stream.

'That's it, that's it. Just as the lad described it.'

As they went closer, excitement turned to alarm. The cottage was roofless, its timbers blackened, a burnt out ruin.

As Faro stood looking at it, Dougie approached. Greeted by Tom he was introduced with: 'Mr Faro was hoping to meet Amy.'

The factor pointed to the cottage. 'She's the luckiest woman alive, old chap. She's been living with her sister in Arbroath for more than a year now.'

Faro found it difficult making polite conversation after this further coincidence of another seemingly inexplicable accident.

'What happened?' he asked.

'Burnt down couple of nights ago. Thunderstorm. Reckon it must have been hit by lightning.'

'I hope there were no casualties.'

'No. It's stood empty since Amy went away. We were thinking of pulling it down. Storm saved us a job,' he added cheerfully.

Now he would never know if the interior had been as Vince described it, thought Faro. But having come this far, he decided to take a chance that Dougie had perhaps encountered the two young people.

Tom's eyes widened as he listened to his friend's bland explanation. 'Actually, I'm a detective, on the track of a pair of runaways. They were seen in this area, and it was thought they might be staying in an empty estate cottage. Tall young chap, curly fair hair, good-looking, early twenties. His companion is a slightly built girl with very distinctive raven black hair, twenty but looks younger.'

He paused to let the information sink in. 'You didn't happen to see them, by any chance?'

The factor shook his head. 'No, I didn't. But that's not surprising, seeing that my cottage is at the other end of the estate.' He tapped his chest. 'I had one of my bad bouts, bronchitis. I was in my bed for a week.'

Nudging Faro in the ribs, he chuckled. 'If they were elopers, I doubt they would be flaunting themselves, anyhow.'

'I just hoped someone might have spotted them.'

'If they were here, then they were in luck, with the laird away to Italy and the house deserted. Most of the servants are allowed home too.'

When they left him, Faro said: 'Damn. Vince called it being discreet but I was sure that in the country stone walls have eyes and ears and foreigners in the district are noted carefully.'

'In the normal way you'd be right,' Tom agreed. 'There's nothing much goes on in the vicinity without it being a talking point in the servants' hall. Hedgerows have ears and empty windows have eyes all right. The folk here are as alert to the passing of strangers as any guard on duty outside Holyrood Palace.'

Tom was silent for a moment. 'Even if you found some-one, what good would all this do, Jeremy? As far as I can see, it wouldn't make one iota of difference to your lad.'

'I realise that. I suppose all I want to do is to prove him right.'

'You've done that. Even if you had a roomful of witnesses that would only prove the Deane girl was a liar. But in the long run, that wouldn't make her change her mind about marrying your lad. And one word of warning, tangling with the Deane family means trouble.'

'So I have heard.'

'Aye, they are powerful enough to do anything they want by bribes or threats – or maybe worse – to close mouths of folk who might be trying to damage their saintly reputation.'

'Are you implying there is something I ought to know, Tom?'

'Perhaps. When I was on the force we had plenty of problems with the family that never reached the public's ears. The lass's mother took her own life, drowned herself in the estate pond over yonder.'

He shrugged. 'I should say that's what was supposed to have happened. But no one was absolutely convinced that she hadn't been given a helping hand. There were other scandals quickly suppressed, pregnant servant girls and so forth, false accusations substantiated by bought witnesses. I shouldn't be telling you this, Jeremy, but I wouldn't be a bit surprised if a lot of money passed hands to buy silences that were really miscarriages of justice.

'If you really want to put the Deane family under the microscope Superintendent Johnston is your man. He wouldn't do it for just anyone but a senior detective has certain privileges.'

'I know him already. We have worked together on cases in the past.'

'Then he knows anything he tells you will go no further. It's well worth a try, Jeremy.'

The two old friends spent the rest of the visit in happy recollection of the past and of the remarkable advances in police methods of detection over the last twenty years.

As Tom saw him on to the Dundee train, Faro thanked him for all his help.

Tom grinned. 'You know what? I'm glad I'm not young and vulnerable any more. At least we've proved that your lad isn't suffering from some delusion caused by overwork, undernourishment and chronic infatuation.'

As the train slid out of the station, Faro found himself remembering Tom's words which again impinged on that other world, still closed to him. The workings of the human mind and its motives were becoming increasingly the concern of Vince's profession.

His own, the detection of crime, was somewhat more direct and based on tangible evidence and clues left at the scene of the crime or carried away by the criminal. A great deal easier to deal with, he decided, than sorting out the intricacies and vagaries of human behaviour.

Perhaps some day . . .

And he settled back to read the newspaper he had bought and had never had time to open.

'Man Falls under Dundee Train.'

With a sickened feeling of renewed horror, he saw the name Hamish McGowan staring up at him.

Chapter Nine

An elderly man, Mr Hamish McGowan of Groat Street, was fatally injured when he slipped and fell under the wheels of an oncoming train in Dundee Railway Station late last night. There were no witnesses to the accident but according to his widow, McGowan was well-known to suffer from dizzy spells.

When they reached Dundee, Faro called in at the station-master's office.

'Tragic, tragic, Inspector. But you were here yourself when we warned him.'

'Warned him?'

'Yes, indeed. About threatening Mr Wilfred Deane.'

'A moment please – what has this to do with Mr Deane? Was he expected off the train?'

The station-master looked vague. 'Oh, I don't know about that, Inspector. Actually it wasn't a passenger train, it was the ten o'clock goods train McGowan fell under, but I expect he was lying in wait as usual.'

'What makes you think that?' demanded Faro.

'Well, he was pacing up and down the platform as he always did and I was trying to keep an eye on him.'

'That must have been difficult for you. Surely it was dark by then.'

'Oh, pitch black. But the platform is always lit by gas lamps.' The station-master frowned, 'Of course, it was very windy too. Perhaps he lost his balance,' he added hopefully.

'When was the next train due?'

'At ten thirty, the last one from Perth.'

It seemed unlikely that McGowan would be pacing the platform half an hour before the local passenger train arrived.

What had brought him to the station at that hour? Did he still intend to murder Wilfred Deane despite all his promises?

Faro frowned. He could have sworn that McGowan was a man of his word. So what happened that night to change his mind?

There was only one way to find out. He remembered the scrap of paper he had in his wallet. He would visit the grieving widow but first he must tell Vince the results of his investigations at Errol.

As he let himself into the dismal lodging, Jean McGonagall was waiting for him, her face glowing with suppressed excitement.

'There's been a constable here. Looking for you, Mr Faro.' She paused dramatically. 'You're to go to the police station directly.'

'Did you tell Dr Laurie?'

She shook her head. 'Couldn't, sir. He's not been in. Never came for his supper either. Probably an accident of some kind.'

Faro tried not to think of what that accident might have been or whether the victim in this case might be Vince himself. Cursing the brevity of the constable's message, which he felt had aged him several years, he hurried in the direction of the police station.

'Yes, Inspector Faro. The Superintendent is waiting for you, sir. He's in his office.'

Superintendent Johnston's smile was a trifle wan. He looked embarrassed as they shook hands.

'Sorry about all this, Faro.'

The Superintendent flourished a piece of paper. 'It seems that your stepson, Dr Laurie, has been in a bit of trouble. Taken into custody.'

'What?' If there was any sense of relief mingled with Faro's astonishment, it was that the lad was at least alive and unhurt.

'Here, read it for yourself,' said the Superintendent. With a sympathetic nod, he added: 'The young fellows these days. Impulsive they are.'

Faro quickly read the note signed by the constable on duty. He had been called to Deane Hall where Dr Vincent Beaumarcher Laurie had been restrained and subsequently put under arrest for 'violent behaviour and abusive language and threatening bodily harm to Mr Wilfred Deane'.

Faro cursed. 'My apologies, sir. This really is too bad. After all his promises of good behaviour too.'

'I gather the young man is enamoured of Miss Deane.' The Superintendent raised his eyes heavenward. 'We must make allowances for infatuations. We older folk have lived long enough to regard falling in love as a temporary state of insanity,' he added with a sigh.

Faro gave him a sharp glance. A married man with six children at the last count, Johnston no doubt spoke from a wealth of experience.

Leaning forward resting his elbows on the desk, the Superintendent said: 'Well, Faro, what are we to do? I am reluctant to have this go any further – the scandal and so forth. We don't want to bring this into the court and neither – to give them credit, for I gather this is not the first offence – do the Deane family.'

Rubbing his chin thoughtfully he added: 'If you could possibly guarantee his behaviour in future, the weight of your reputation will be enough to placate them, I fancy.' And when Faro looked doubtful, 'They are showing considerable patience and forbearing, you know. So is this young lady who is being constantly harassed. Do you think you could talk some sense into the lad?'

He frowned over the constable's note again as if there was something he might have missed the first time. 'I

90

gather the damage to property included the smashing of a window and a valuable vase in the hall. Chinese it was, cost a hundred pounds—'

Faro groaned. What on earth had possessed Vince to behave in this ridiculous manner? 'I will settle the account. And you have my word that I will do my very best to ensure that my stepson keeps well away from Deane Hall in future.'

As they shook hands, Johnston smiled. He looked relieved. 'It was good to see you again, Faro. Look, let's have dinner together. I'll consult the wife and see what we have on. Staying long?'

'Alas, no. I'm due back at the Central Office early next week.'

'In that case we had better make it lunch at my club tomorrow. Pity you're going so soon.'

It was indeed, thought Faro, just three days to sort out the mess Vince was making of his life. Almost certain that Vince would lose his job over this fiasco and, what was worse, would not be given a reference, Faro realised there was a distinct possibility that he would not be returning to Edinburgh alone.

The real tragedy was that Vince's reckless behaviour might have cost him his future as a doctor, for Faro could not imagine Sir Arnold, once he heard about this evening's events, ever letting the young madman set foot across his threshold to threaten his family and terrify his granddaughter.

Accompanying him to the door, the Superintendent said: 'Until tomorrow, then?' And with a final sympathetic smile, 'As I said before, it's a pity you can't stay around until this business blows over. We'd all be happier if you were keeping an eye on the lad.'

'And so would I, but I can't be keeper to a grown man. He has to lead his own life. For better or for worse.'

'Caution him as best you can, Faro. If he does it again or makes a nuisance of himself in any way we'll have to

91

put him inside. And if it comes to fisticuffs, as you well know, the scandal could finish him. Impress that upon him and for God's sake tell him to grow up. He'll soon meet someone else. There's better fish in the sea . . . '

But the time-worn cliché didn't console Faro or Vince, or put either of them in a better frame of mind.

Vince was pathetically eager to see him, a study in relief when he saw his stepfather walking down towards the cell where he was under guard.

Faro's hopes, however, sank to zero when his stepson emerged. Always so spruce and elegant, now unkempt, unshaven, and looking as if he hadn't slept for several days, he had obviously been drinking heavily.

Taking him firmly by the arm and saying, 'We'll talk later,' Faro marched him out of the police station. Once outside, he could restrain himself no longer. 'For God's sake, Vince, you look terrible.'

'And disgusting, don't I? Frankly I don't care what I look like, I don't care about anything any more. Particularly at this moment, whether I live or die—'

'That's your decision,' said Faro coldly, momentarily lacking his usual compassion and understanding. 'I've just come from a harrowing interview with the Superintendent.'

'So you know all about my shocking behaviour.'

He didn't sound contrite in the least. However, the expression on Faro's face as he looked in his direction halted him. As of old, he knew when he had gone too far.

'I'm sorry, Stepfather, really I am. Getting you involved like this.'

'And so you should be. You haven't given me a red face before anyone since your schooldays. And now I find myself having to guarantee your good behaviour. It really isn't good enough, after all your promises.'

'I've said I'm sorry—'

'Then I'd like to see you act like it, instead of being an impulsive young fool and getting the police into all this. If you hadn't had me on hand, you'd be cooling your heels in that prison cell with the door locked until your case came up before the court. Don't you realise what you're doing?'

Vince was silent and Faro stopped in his tracks, pulled him roughly by the shoulders to face him. 'Look, lad, before we go any further I want your word, your solemn promise, now, before I leave Dundee, that you will stay away from Rachel Deane.'

Faro hadn't spoken so severely to his stepson since the latter was nine years old and had played truant from school. He might have grown up but that look of mutinous hostility carried Faro right back through the years. To the early days of his marriage to Vince's mother Lizzie when he had been faced by the implacable hatred of her illegitimate son.

Now almost as soon as he had noticed it, it was gone, replaced by Vince's most charming smile, albeit apologetic and a trifle wan. 'All right, Stepfather. I give you my word. Here's my hand on it. No more assaults upon Deane Hall. Although I'd like to kill Wilfred Deane. Smug smiling bastard. Oh, I'm sorry, Stepfather.'

'Being sorry is not enough. Did you ever look ahead for one moment and consider the fact that your infantile behaviour might cost you your post here with Deane's and seriously jeopardise any future one you might consider applying for? Can you in all honesty see them giving you a reference after such atrocious behaviour?'

Vince wilted under his stepfather's cold anger. 'I just wanted to try once more. That was all. I was very polite. But this time Wilfred Deane opened the door and said that Rachel was not at home and that if I continued these harassments then they would call the police.'

'Which he was quite at liberty to do if he felt they were being harassed.'

Vince ignored that. 'I argued with him, but I didn't lay a hand on him.' He clenched his fists, remembering. 'I could have choked the smug bastard, smiling at me,

93

daring me to make a move. I called out Rachel's name, hoping she would hear and come and help me. Then the butler took over and between them they threw me out bodily. As for Rachel, she had never showed her face. Not a sign of her. But she was at home.'

'How do you know that?' Faro demanded sharply.

'They were lying. As I picked myself up from the drive, I saw her at one of the upstairs windows. Watching me. Never lifting a finger in protest. That was too much. I'm afraid I assaulted the front door and when no one came, I threw a stone through the window. You know the rest,' he said shamefacedly. 'Dear God, what am I to do?'

'Stay away from Deane Hall, for a start.'

Faro was furious. Anyone but Vince could see with half an eye that the girl no longer cared for him. Whatever motives had led her to that brief infatuation were now over and she deeply regretted her lapse from virtue.

Again he found himself wondering whether some quirk in her mind they did not fully understand had led her to seek an amorous adventure with her grandfather's handsome young doctor.

However, when she realised that his intentions were serious, she had coldly calculated, or had been made by her family to calculate, that she could not possibly exchange her life of luxury and plenty at Deane Hall for something which would seem to her by comparison only a little better than the squalor in which their workers lived.

As Paton's Lane approached, Faro said: 'You were speaking the truth. About the cottage, I mean. At least I've proved that. I've been to Errol for the day.'

Vince looked up, suddenly hopeful. 'You have? Oh thank you, Stepfather. Thank you. Did you see Rachel's old nurse? Did she tell you?'

Faro opened the door of his room. 'Sit down, lad.' It was very puzzling and to avoid arousing Vince's wrath with probing questions he had to proceed with great caution. At the end of his account Vince shook his head dully.

'I think I'll go to bed, Stepfather. Will you excuse me? This has been quite a day and I don't think I'm capable of coherent thought any more.'

As his stepson left, he embraced him: 'There, there, lad. Don't worry. We'll sort it all out.'

Vince smiled. 'Thank you, Stepfather. What was it I used to say when I was a little chap? I'll try to be a credit to you.'

'Something like that. Sleep well, lad.'

Putting his head round the door, Vince asked: 'Is it true? Must you go back to Edinburgh so soon?' The question was followed by a look of disappointment and distress when Faro replied: 'Monday afternoon. Sharp.'

Vince swore. 'Now you'll never meet Rachel. Now you'll never know or understand how I adore her. And yet it's just as well. I guessed at that first meeting that you weren't terribly impressed,' he added with a shrewd glance.

'We didn't have much chance to get acquainted,' said Faro uncomfortably, heartily glad that it was unlikely he'd have the embarrassment of a second encounter.

In that as in so many things concerning Vince and Rachel Deane, he was to be completely mistaken.

Chapter Ten

Promises, it seemed to Faro just then, were easy to make and easy to break. However, it was a very shame-faced Vince he met at breakfast next morning.

'I promise not to get into any more trouble, Stepfather. You have my word.'

You have my word. McGowan had said that. Yet only twenty-four hours later he had been back at Dundee Station, pacing the platform, a madman stalking his quarry once again.

Perhaps it would be better to shrug off the whole incident, but Faro's sense of fair play demanded some sort of explanation for McGowan's rash behaviour which had cost him his life.

'How do I get to Groat Street?' And as Vince gave him directions he said, 'I'm hoping to see McGowan's widow.'

'McGowan? The man who was threatening Wilfred Deane?'

'The man who believed that his son's death was no accident and whose daughter-in-law has mysteriously disappeared.'

'I can well see that he felt justified in wishing to kill Deane,' said Vince grimly.

At the door, Faro turned. 'Have you half an hour to spare? Good. Would you care to accompany me?'

In Groat Street they climbed the winding stone stairs of a tenement similar in every way to the one they had left in Paton's Lane.

The door was opened by a young woman in mourning dress.

'I have come to pay my condolences to Mrs McGowan,' said Faro, wondering how he was to explain that he was a detective.

The young woman shook her head. 'Ma's no' very well. She's in her bed. I canna get her to see the doctor and her so poorly.'

Vince smiled and stepped forward. 'Perhaps I can help. I am the doctor at Deane's.'

'Oh sir, would you take a look at her? Her heart has always been bad but this shock of Da being killed—' She shook her head and left the sentence unfinished.

Mrs McGowan lay in the bed in the kitchen recess since the bedroom was occupied by her husband's coffin. Even to Faro's eyes she did look very poorly indeed. As Vince bent over her, he took a seat at the table opposite McGowan's daughter.

'Have you any idea how this dreadful accident happened?'

'All I could get from Ma was that he had someone to meet. He told her it wouldna' take long and that he'd be back for his supper. The next thing she knew was the police at the door.'

Her eyes filled with tears and she left him abruptly to refill the kettle at the kitchen sink. 'You'll both have a cup of tea?'

Vince, having completed his examination, said: 'She is very weak but there is no immediate cause for alarm. Plenty of rest and good nourishing food. I am sure you know better than anyone how to take good care of your mother,' he added with a smile.

The young woman shrugged, pouring out the tea. 'I may not be staying very long. I'm living in Liverpool now. It is just by chance that I happen to be here at all, on the way back from my young sister's wedding.' And glancing towards the bed:

'She's no' my ma. I was married to Charlie McGowan.'

97

So this was the missing widow.

'Your father-in-law was very anxious about you.'

'I know and I'm sorry about that. You see, I couldn't really tell them. They'd have been that upset. They thought Charlie and me were happy together, but that wasn't the way of it at all. I had already decided to leave him. I went a couple of days before the accident.'

She gave a shrug of distaste. 'He was going with another woman, some lass he worked with and I'd gone back to my lad that I let down to marry Charlie. I left a letter, but he must never have told his folks. Too ashamed, because they thought the world of him.

'I only heard through my sister that he was dead. I got a shock, I can tell you. I didn't want to come here. I was too embarrassed to explain it all. However, when I was home this time, my folks told me that I should come and see the McGowans because they thought something had happened to me. Well, something had,' she added grimly, 'but not what they thought.'

She sighed. 'Now at least poor Pa McGowan will never know the truth about us. I'm glad he's been spared that.'

They left shortly afterwards, Vince promising to look in and see Mrs McGowan again.

'Well, what do you make of that, Stepfather?'

'One missing woman accounted for, and with a simple explanation for her movements.'

'After that, I shouldn't be in the least surprised if the fair Kathleen walks into Paton's Lane hale and hearty one day.'

Faro smiled. 'You will let me know?'

'I will indeed. At least this is one mystery happily solved.'

'One mystery that existed only in poor McGowan's mind.'

Was that the answer? Had McGowan meant to fall under that train, thought Faro as he walked to the club where he was meeting Superintendent Johnston for lunch, the one person who might be able to offer some discreet and helpful advice regarding the Deane family. At the end of a meal, with more sirloin of beef inside him than a starving Dundee family saw in a year, thought Faro guiltily, he realised there would never be a better moment to question the now mellow Superintendent.

As they sipped their brandy, he said, 'I wonder if you could give me some confidential information.'

'Willingly, if I can.' Johnston smiled benignly.

'It's about the Deane family.'

'Indeed.' Faro felt that a shadow of reserve had come over his friend's manner. 'What was it you wanted to know?' was the cautious response.

'Oh, just something of their family history.'

The Superintendent leaned forward. 'Are your people on to this?' he demanded sharply.

'I'm not sure what you mean.'

'Your special branch. Have they got wind of it?'

'Wind of what?'

Johnston leaned back in his chair with a sigh of relief. 'I'm not sure whether I should talk about this, even to you, although there's nobody I'd trust more in normal circumstances.'

He hesitated before continuing. 'I dare say it will all come out in the not too distant future but the position regarding Deane's is that we're investigating a massive case of fraud concerning the building of the bridge. We're in the very early stages and we don't want to scare anyone off.'

He laughed uneasily. 'It gave me quite a nasty turn when I thought the Edinburgh Police were on to it.'

Faro shook his head. 'No. My reason is rather more personal.'

'I should have realised that. Your stepson, of course.'

Faro broke a silence that threatened to be lengthy. 'Now you've aroused my curiosity, sir. I have always understood that Deane was the soul of respectability, a pillar of society and a public benefactor.'

'So did everyone else, until recently. As you know

they have the contract for the bridge. Fought tooth and nail to get it, plenty of competitors too. Even without undercutting everyone else in the field, they were the obvious choice, with their background – the Baron of Broughty and all that sort of thing.'

Again he paused so long that Faro prompted him. 'Do go on.'

Johnston nodded in the manner of a man who comes to a sudden decision. 'Well, things seemed to be fine at the beginning and then there was a series of misfortunes. The bridge was to be finished in two years. Any fool could see that it wasn't possible, but lately there have been a staggering number of accidents.'

'Vince is the factory doctor, so I know something of them.'

'Well, the accidents seem to have been due to shoddy materials and poor workmanship – gantries collapsing, piers sunk without careful knowledge of the rock formation. As you've maybe heard, the Tay is a tricky river at the best of times, subject to violent storms and high winds which haven't helped much.'

Faro smiled. 'I've experienced several kinds of remarkable weather in the few days I've been here.'

Johnston nodded. 'One of our detectives whose nephew was lost decided to take a further look, employing some plain-clothes men as navvies. The things the humble constable has to take in his stride. Anyway, he discovered that the sound materials which had been ordered and paid for had often been replaced by cheaper, less substantial and, indeed, often inferior ones.'

He tapped his fingers against his glass. 'In other words, Faro, someone has been making a hefty packet out of the enterprise. But this is no ordinary fraud, this is tantamount to murder when you consider the lives that have been endangered.'

It was a shocking story and confirmed what McGowan had told him of his son's discovery.

'This man McGowan who fell under the train—'

100

Johnston nodded and Faro continued: 'He told me that his son who worked in the finance department suspected fraudulent dealings.'

'Precisely. It was from him we received our first inklings.'

'Were you not suspicious then, when he so conveniently met with an accident on the bridge?'

'Of course we were. First the man Simms and then young McGowan. The two prime witnesses in a fraud enquiry.'

'Then why didn't you do something about it?' asked Faro angrily.

'Look, Faro, you know the rules as well as I do. They were both dead and we had nothing yet to prove our suspicions. But if we stormed in with accusations at this delicate stage, we'd alert whoever was guilty. Then Simms and McGowan would have died in vain.'

His reasoning didn't please Faro. This wasn't the way he worked even if there was a kind of logic about it. 'Can nothing be done about the bridge at this stage?'

'Not without tearing down the whole structure and starting again. And we'd certainly never be able to convince the shareholders that we were acting in the passengers' best interests. Or that poorer materials than those ordered had been used and that careless measurements had been made. They would simply laugh at us. After all, they have big money at stake. And that is what counts. Not human lives, Faro. Money and secure investments.'

'But if this goes on and the bridge is ever completed, you realise the danger. A trainload of passengers. My God, to sit back and do nothing is quite unthinkable.'

'We could all be wrong, you know. It is maybe not as serious as it sounds. We can do nothing meantime but if this fraud is proved then we will certainly insist that the work so far be properly reinforced to make it doubly secure.'

'Let us hope that it isn't too late and that your bridge isn't already doomed.'

Johnston frowned. 'Of course, it will cause a lot of bother. Delaying completion for a few more years will greatly distress the shareholders.'

'Damn the shareholders. What do their feelings matter when the whole bridge may fall in the first storm and take a full passenger train with it?' Faro shuddered. 'Dear God, it doesn't bear thinking about.'

'We've already been warned about that.' A moment later Johnston added casually. 'Not psychic by any chance, are you, Inspector?'

'Not that I admit to.'

'Then you needn't worry. My mother was Highland and I get the odd quiver now and again. One of our famous citizens was the Seer of Gourdie.'

'Yes, I've heard of him.'

'He was remarkably accurate about his own and other people's lives, foretelling his own death and other major, less personal events.'

'And he predicted that this rainbow bridge would fall. I heard about that.'

Johnston nodded. 'Of course, everyone laughed at such an idea. Took refuge in the knowledge that old Patrick Matthews was born in the eighteenth century. What could a man with old-fashioned ideas possibly understand about the marvels of modern progress and science?' Johnston paused and regarded him grimly. 'I just hope he's wrong.'

'And if he's right, that there's no train going across at the time it falls,' Faro repeated in worried tones, for the enormity of Johnston's revelations had thrust all else aside.

While the waiter replenished their glasses, Johnston asked: 'How is your stepson today? Has he recovered from his temporary experience of police hospitality?' he added with a grin.

'I hope so. I gave him a good talking to and extracted a promise that he would keep away from Deane Hall.'

Johnston sat back in his chair. 'Poor lad. If it isn't

too late I'd implore him to steer clear of Rachel Deane. Forget about her.'

'How so?' demanded Faro sharply.

The Superintendent shrugged. 'Because the lass isn't – well, stable, let's say. She has a family history of mental illness, her mother and father were first cousins and Mrs Deane committed suicide while the lass was still a bairn.'

'One of my friends, Tom Elgin, whom you may remember, told me about that when I was visiting him.'

The Superintendent nodded. 'As is often the case in these close-knit families, they waver between producing brilliant sons and simpletons.'

'Do you know Miss Deane personally?'

'We've visited the house socially through the years. And I've never been left with a very good impression. Rude, wild, and liable to throw the soup at the maid if it didn't please her. The kind that makes you grind your teeth and if there wasn't the excuse of some kind of mental disturbance, then you'd be tempted to take the hairbrush to her backside.'

'Has she ever been under restraint?'

'You mean put away? No, that possibility has never been raised. Not strictly necessary in her case since she has never been a danger, so far as I have heard, to anyone but herself. If she'd been in poorer circumstances there might have been some reason, but fortunately for her, Deane Hall is a big place. When she has these erratic outbursts from time to time, I gather she can be effectively put under restraint at home.'

'But this girl is the heiress, the whole of Deane's fortune comes to her as the only offspring.'

'That has been taken care of. Wilfred Deane, her second cousin, is in charge of the family finances and in fact is virtually top man since Sir Arnold's illness. He wants to marry her. Did your stepson mention that?'

'No. First I've heard of it.'

'Well, give the girl her due, she is not to be pushed into marriage either. Just as well,' said Johnston.

'You mean—'

'If this embezzlement business is proved, Wilfred Deane is likely to be spending some years behind bars.'

What an unholy mess. Faro walked back to Paton's Lane feeling considerably upset. How could he tell Vince that Rachel Deane had obviously escaped her supervised seclusion in Deane Hall only long enough to indulge her appetite for romance? Perhaps any man would have done just as well. The butler for instance.

But how to tell his lovesick stepson that his first great love, the consummation of his passion, had been with a girl with a family history of madness. A girl he could never hope to make his wife, even if she had not denied ever knowing him.

Johnston's revelations explained her violent reaction but how could he tactfully warn Vince? He rephrased over and over the words he would need and discarded them all as totally inadequate consolation for Vince in his present state of mind.

Gloomily aware that by now his stepson might have another pressing problem, in the form of dismissal from his situation as factory doctor, he climbed the stairs to their lodging.

Vince bounded towards him, beaming with delight. But the letter in his hand was the last that Faro expected.

'Guess what, Stepfather. I've had a note from Rachel. I knew – I told you – it was all her family's doing. And I was right. She wants me to meet her. I knew she still loves me. And she does.' He flourished a piece of paper. 'Read that. Read it. Now you'll be convinced.'

And Faro realised that any words of warning he might care to offer were now too late.

Chapter Eleven

Dearest Vince. Meet me at Magdalen Green (where we met once before by the bridge) at 7 this evening. I will explain everything then. Do not fail me. I love you. Your Rachel.

Faro handed the note back. He was speechless.

'Well, Stepfather. What do you think of that?' demanded Vince triumphantly.

Highly suspicious were the first two words that occurred to Faro. He could not bring himself to respond to Vince's enthusiasm and utter the encouragement expected of him. Somewhat hesitantly, he said 'I presume there is no doubt that this is Rachel's handwriting?'

'Really, Stepfather,' was the scornful rejoinder, 'I do know her handwriting. For heaven's sake, this is their crested notepaper, too. And I have other notes from her. Here,' he added taking out his pocket case. 'Read them if you wish. Check them carefully,' he added stiffly.

'No need for that, lad.'

'Thank you.' Vince's words were tinged with sarcasm as he replaced the notes, but on his lips was a dreamlike smile. Now that he believed Rachel Deane loved him, he was ready, even eager, to forget all the indignities she had heaped upon him. It was as if the last two days had never happened and Vince was about to rush headlong into the fantasy world they, or most likely he, had created.

'I can hardly believe it, after all that has happened.'

Neither can I, lad. Neither can I, thought Faro gloomily.

'It's like a miracle.'

A miracle or another cruel trick to destroy his stepson, he thought listening to Vince now full of plans and speculations, all highly romantic and, Faro decided, highly impractical.

'Her grandfather dotes upon her and I have not the least doubt that she has persuaded him to let us marry. Don't you agree?' And not waiting for a reply, 'That swine Wilfred must have been the stumbling block. No doubt she will tell me all about it—'

Faro cut him short. 'Wait a moment, lad. Why all the secrecy? If she has the family approval, surely she or her grandfather might have invited you up to the house?'

He had to do his best to warn Vince that all might not be as he anticipated. He succeeded, for Vince looked suddenly thoughtful.

'Yes, that is a possibility I hadn't considered. Another is that she is making her escape from Deane Hall and wishes us to elope. That is something we have discussed before, in happier days,' he added wistfully. 'After all, she will be of age in two weeks' time—'

The more Faro listened, the more convinced he became that the note from Rachel and the whole situation it conjured up were deeply suspicious. A situation that Vince, in a sane mood, would have regarded with the utmost caution.

Watching his stepson prepare for the meeting, whistling happily, filled Faro with ominous dread that this time Vince himself might be in danger. When he emerged shaved and well-groomed, wearing his best suit and cravat, every trace of any recent despondency had vanished completely. Young and handsome, he was revitalised by his lost love returned.

At six thirty the sky clouded over. The weather had changed, a squally wind followed by heavy rain indicated that a storm was blowing up the Tay.

106

Vince mistook his stepfather's sombre countenance for anxiety about the weather. 'How exasperating!'

It was just a few minutes' walk from Paton's Lane to Magdalen Green but on a night like this, with forebodings of disaster pricking like daggers in his mind, Faro came to a sudden decision. 'We'll need to take a carriage. And I'm coming with you.'

'But – but there is absolutely no necessity—'

'It's all right, lad, I promise not to intrude. I shall remain discreetly inside the carriage.' And in a flash of pure invention, 'You see, it's just occurred to me that if you're eloping, the assistance of a third party might be extremely useful.'

'Well done, Stepfather. It never entered my head. You do think of everything, don't you?'

Hiring carriages on the busy main road from the railway station were readily accessible. At five minutes to seven they reached Magdalen Green. As the road near the bridge offered little shelter but a large quantity of mud underfoot, the cab driver agreed that for another shilling they might wait inside the carriage.

Those last few minutes were an eternity for Vince and a gnawing anxiety for his stepfather. The bridge was empty of workmen now, with gaslight flares to help the night-watchman in his task.

The swaying lanterns reflected the ghostly dark shapes of the piers of the bridge. No longer echoing with the sound of daytime hammerings, the creak and groan of cranes and pulleys as they elevated their heavy baskets to the higher platforms, only the wind whistled eerily, rustling up a tide which tugged and dragged at the half-finished girders.

Seven o'clock struck and faded away, but there was no sign of Rachel.

As for Faro, he became more convinced with every passing moment that Rachel herself would not appear, as his sinking heart told him that this had been yet another cruel practical joke at Vince's expense.

107

Nevertheless, he was now watchful, alert to possible danger. If that note had been a ruse to lure Vince to this lonely place, then the lad might be in mortal peril, with paid assassins lurking in the dark shadows of the bridge.

They were in for a surprise, he thought grimly, feeling triumphant and thankful that he had spoilt their plan by accompanying Vince to this assignation. He and Vince had been in many similar scrapes and they had acquitted themselves nobly, more than a match for their adversaries. Wishing he had not left his pistol in Edinburgh, he now looked for something that might be used in defence as well as their own fists.

In the flickering gaslight, he could see by Vince's eager face that he had not the least suspicion that anything was amiss. Hopeful, his spirits buoyant, he whistled under his breath.

'This carriage was a good idea of yours, Stepfather. We would be getting very wet indeed, wouldn't we?'

Through the window which they had reeled down, they could see the darkness of the river speckled with white horses and Faro remembered ominously Shakespeare's 'Seas do laugh, show white, when rocks are near.'

The rain had ceased, revealing a full moon drifting through occasional breaks in the clouds. Faro glanced at Vince. Was he remembering its effects on lunatic patients? And a voice inside whispered: 'How then will it affect Rachel Deane?'

Now the occasional boom of sea lapping the shore competed with an eldritch wind, rattling here and there some loose segment on the piers above their heads.

Seven fifteen struck from a church clock nearby and Faro was about to suggest that they wait no longer, when Vince seized his arm:

'Listen.'

A closed carriage approached.

Faro leaned forward expectantly. Could it be Rachel? 'There she is. There she is.'

But the carriage swept past them and stopped twenty yards further down the road near the bridge.

'It must be her. Of course, she was expecting me to be on foot.' He leaped out. 'Rachel, Rachel. Over here.'

Faro watched from the window as Vince ran down the road to greet the girl who emerged from the carriage.

Now she was close enough for Faro to observe in the wavering gaslight that she was in a state of considerable excitement, or distress, or apprehension. Considering the inclement weather she was most inadequately clad, he thought. A light shawl only partially covered a plain dark dress, her hair hidden under a tall bonnet tied firmly under her chin. And that fretful wind, tearing at her gown, revealed light slippers.

Faro sighed. She carried only a small reticule over her wrist, hardly the luggage of a young lady intending to elope. Here was no triumphant mistress, blessed with family approval, coming to meet her lover. Appearances hinted that her departure from Deane Hall had been in some confusion and haste and that she wished to keep her assignation secret.

Vince had reached her side, arms outstretched in a lover's embrace. But again all was not well. Over Vince's shoulder she was staring at the carriage. She had caught sight of Faro and he saw her thrust Vince away so savagely that he staggered off balance and slipped on the wet road.

'Get away from me,' she cried. 'Leave me alone.'

Taken aback by the violence of the girl's reaction, Faro was never quite certain what happened next. Even as he sprang from the carriage to assist Vince to his feet, Rachel Deane ran swiftly down the road.

Vince was doubled up, winded, clutching his stomach. It was obvious, thought Faro grimly, that the innocent Miss Rachel knew something about self-defence too.

'Oh God, why did she do that? I didn't mean to upset her. Where is she? Tell her to come back.'

The gas flares illuminated her flight down the road

towards the bridge. Once a cab came along and for a moment she seemed to be trying to make it stop. Then changing her mind she ran alongside the wooden fence. Some six feet high, its purpose was to keep at bay inquisitive children and deter any unauthorised persons from exploring the unfinished bridge.

As they followed her, even the elements turned against them.

With heavy rain renewed and driving into their faces, by the time they reached the gate and discovered it was locked, Rachel Deane had found another entrance.

A tiny figure in a billowing gown, she was already high above their heads, climbing steadily the swaying ladder on the bridge's first pier.

Chapter Twelve

As Vince shook the gates, shouting: 'Rachel, Rachel, come back,' Faro examined the padlock.

'She didn't go in here. There must be some other way in.'

They found it easily. A few yards away, a broken plank in the fence. A narrow gap that only a very slender girl could have contemplated.

As Vince and Faro tried to squeeze through, a night-watchman, alerted by the voices raised above the gale, appeared from his hut. He carried a lantern and was yawning, obviously just awake.

'What's going on?' he demanded sleepily. 'No one's allowed to come in here.'

'Let us in. Open the door, I am a doctor,' said Vince.

The man glared at him and shook his head obstinately. 'Whatever you are, I canna open that gate without proper authority. More than my job's worth.'

'So is sleeping on duty,' snapped Vince.

'Is that so—'

'Stop arguing,' Faro interrupted. 'Look over there, a girl is climbing on to the bridge.'

'A girl? You must be mistaken. No one's come in here without me seeing them—'

'Use your eyes, man. Over there!'

The watchman raised his lantern. 'She canna do that,' he cried indignantly. 'It's not allowed. She'll get into an awfa' row for that—'

'For heaven's sake, man, don't you see, she's in danger.

111

She could fall to her death, if we don't stop her. Now will you unlock this door?'

As the man withdrew his set of keys, he said: 'I still don't see how she got in—'

'She came through a hole in the fence. Down there.'

The watchman sidled down towards the gap and inspected it, frowning. 'Well now, I'd better get that fixed. Some laddies must have been up to mischief. There'll be trouble when Mr Deane finds out. Very safety conscious, he is.'

'For God's sake, will you open this door,' said Vince.

'Steady on there, sir. Steady on.' And misinterpreting Vince's desperation he said: 'Been at the bottle, have you, laddie? Go home and sleep it off.'

As Vince shook the gate savagely once again, he added sternly, 'Now, now, damage Deane's property and I'll need to get the polis to you.'

That was the key. Cursing himself for not having thought of it before, Faro said: 'I'm an Inspector of Police, and Superintendent Johnston will vouch for me. Dr Laurie here works for Deane's.'

The watchman, who was considerably smaller and slighter than the two men who faced him, now held the lantern high and peered into their faces. 'Dr Laurie. So you are. So you are, sir. You should have said so. I expect it'll be all right to let you in.'

And unlocking the gate, he added sympathetically, 'One of your escaped patients is it, sir?'

But Vince and Faro had pushed past him and were already in headlong pursuit of Rachel. His vociferous protests followed as he tried vainly to keep up with them.

'Wait a minute, gentlemen. I'll need to come with you. I'm not supposed to let anyone on the bridge. It's more than my job's worth.'

But neither heeded him.

'Look. Look. Up there.'

In the gaslight's feeble flare they saw Rachel Deane,

112

now thirty feet above them, a tiny windswept figure clinging to the ironwork. She had reached the first platform of the pier.

'Rachel. For God's sake, come back—'

For a moment she paused, a pale face looked down at them.

'Stay there, Rachel. Don't move. I'm coming up.'

Horrified, Faro caught up with Vince at the base of the ladder. Rachel had discarded her satin slippers to make her climb easier, abandoning her reticule to free her hands. Vince thrust the slippers into his pocket and Faro seized the reticule as they began their ascent of the frail ladder.

'Come back, come back,' shouted the watchman. 'It'll no' hold the lot of you. You'll all be killed.'

Vince remained where he was looking upwards. Rachel had disappeared momentarily, concealed by the frail wooden shield erected to protect workmen from the worst of the weather.

'Wait there, Rachel. It's all right. I'll be with you—'

Even as Vince spoke, she reappeared and began a steady and rapid climb towards the second platform some eighty feet above their heads.

'Rachel, Rachel. Stop, for God's sake, stop.'

But Vince's plea, even if she heard it, did not deter her from her purpose. Now far behind Vince, Faro sighed with relief as he saw her reach the second frail shelter in safety.

'You can't go any further, Rachel. Please stay there.'

He heard the terror and agony in Vince's voice as with one faint cry, Rachel hurtled downwards past them.

Clinging to the ironwork, they felt the violent movement of air as her dark gown billowing out transformed her into some gigantic winged bird.

A second later, the turbulent waters of the Tay blossomed into a white rose of death to receive her. Then the blackness closed over once more and all was still.

Knowing that she could stay alive only seconds in

113

those icy waters, both men began sliding, scrambling down the ironwork, oblivious of torn clothes, bruised and bleeding hands.

On firm ground again, Vince cried out, 'Oh God – oh God –' and discarding his coat raced towards the water's edge.

Faro followed, his mind working coldly, his intention at all costs to prevent Vince from plunging into that swift-moving river with some mad idea of saving Rachel Deane. She was past saving. She could not have survived that terrible fall. As for Vince, an indifferent swimmer at the best of times, any attempt at rescue and he too would be a dead man.

'Let me go to her, damn you, damn you.' But Faro held him firm.

'No. No, I beg you – don't.' As they struggled, Vince cursing, Faro pleading, imploring, the watchman panted alongside.

'See, there's a rowing boat down yonder. Take it. I'll go and get help,' he yelled.

Vince and Faro sprang down the pebbled beach, pushed out the boat, leaped in and seized an oar each. Even with two strong men rowing for dear life, the river almost won that bitter struggle. At last they were near the spot where Rachel had fallen. Or had jumped into the dark waters.

Steadying the boat against the vicious tide, they circled, calling her name.

'Rachel. Rachel.'

But even Vince now knew that the battle was lost. Even if she had survived the fall, too much time had now elapsed. There was no longer the faintest possibility of finding her still alive.

A shadow floated towards them. A body, thought Faro for a heart-stopping moment, as he leaned over and fished out a shawl.

Wordlessly he handed it to Vince who clutched that pathetically sodden garment Rachel had worn. Hugging it to him, he sobbed, whispering her name over and over.

'Rachel, Rachel. Why – why? In God's name – why?'

And still with all hope vanquished, they could not return to the shore. Round and round they rowed the boat, stopping now and then to stare at the waters, at some imagined floating object.

Time had ceased to exist. They were both numb with cold and speechless with shock and horror, when Faro became aware that other vessels had joined them in the search.

A voice called from the dark shadow of a deck above their heads. The lifeboat from Broughty Ferry. 'We'll take over, lads. You return to shore. It's too dangerous. There's a gale blowing up.'

Vince shook his head, shouted: 'No. No. We are going to find her.'

Faro, dazed, realised that his feet and trouser legs were sodden. The boat was already half full of water. He began to steer for the shore.

'We'll get another boat, lad. Yes, we'll go on searching. But not in this one. See, we're sinking rapidly.' Raising his voice against the wind, he shouted down Vince's protests.

As they struck the pebbled beach again, he glanced up at the bridge. It was no longer deserted, there were many lights now as workmen in overalls swarmed over the girders holding flickering torches to assist in the search.

Two workmen in overalls were approaching the very spot where Rachel had fallen, from all appearances carrying out a minute inspection.

Faro cursed. And no doubt getting rid of any damning evidence as to what had caused Rachel's death-fall, he thought, following Vince along the river edge in quest of another rowboat.

Suddenly a shout from the lifeboat about twenty yards from the shore. Torches moved in closer and they watched, sick with horror, as a sodden shapeless mass was pulled aboard.

The lifeless body of Rachel Deane.

'Rachel,' Vince screamed, lunging towards the water.

'No. No, lad,' said Faro and held his stepson, sobbing, while the boat with its dread burden drew ashore.

A small crowd had already gathered and Vince wrenched himself free of his stepfather's restraining arms. Head held high, he waded out into the shallows. From the boatman he gently took Rachel and carried her across to the greensward.

She looked so small, thought Faro, as if death had already diminished her. Tiny feet and hands, the gown clinging to the outlines of a childlike body, the bonnet drenched and shapeless but still tied firmly beneath her chin.

Chafing her hands and feet, Vince put his hands into his pockets and drawing out the satin slippers she had abandoned for that fateful climb, he tried to replace them on her feet, so stiff and cold and unyielding.

The alert had been given, the police van and an assortment of carriages were arriving as Vince bent over her and with considerable difficulty tried to untie her bonnet strings.

At last he succeeded and tenderly he spread out her dark hair, like a mantle about her shoulders. And it seemed to Faro, fighting back his own tears, that ruffled by the wind it was the only part of Rachel Deane that moved and lived.

Suddenly the watchers were pushed aside.

'Let me through. Let me through.'

Faro recognised the newcomer as Wilfred Deane, who took one look at the still form of Rachel and dropped on his knees beside her.

'Oh dear God – dear God,' he cried as thrusting Vince away, he took over, trying in vain to chafe life back into her cold hands.

Vince watched him. 'Too late. You are too late,' he said dully.

Deane looked up, recognised him and sprang to his feet. 'Damn you, Laurie, this is all your doing. I might have

116

guessed you had a hand in it. If you'd left her alone, none of this would have ever happened. Dear God, to take her own life.'

Deane swayed where he stood, his face ghastly in the pale light as two constables came forward with a stretcher.

'I will go with her,' said Vince.

Deane seized his arm. 'Oh no, you will not. You have done enough, damn you.'

'I'm a doctor—'

'A fine doctor. More like an executioner. Her murderer, that's what you are.' His voice rose to a screech. 'A callous brutal murderer. And, mark my words, you would hang for this night's work, yes hang, if I had my way—'

His face contorted with hate, Deane lunged forward. Faro seized Vince's arm and Deane's fist hit thin air.

'Gentlemen, gentlemen, I beg you. This won't get you anywhere,' he said desperately. 'Try to be calm, for God's sake.'

Deane turned on him ferociously. 'We tried to warn him that my poor cousin was unbalanced.'

'She was not—'

'She was unbalanced,' Deane said slowly, 'and has been subject to fits of irresponsible behaviour since childhood. We all knew about it and tried to keep her from emotional involvements.' With a shake of his head, he added: 'We were warned long ago that such could throw her over the brink into madness—'

'You lie – you lie,' screamed Vince. 'I don't believe it – I won't—'

Deane laughed harshly. 'Then you had better try to believe it. Because you're going to have to live with this night's work for the rest of your life. You were in love with a madwoman.'

And turning on his heel to follow the stretcher back through the crowd to the police van, he looked at Vince and said sadly: 'We have that in common. So was I.'

The crowd moved nearer with sympathetic murmurs.

117

'Best get yourselves home. Out of those wet clothes. Catch your deaths. Aye, a good dram or two to warm ye.'

A police carriage rolled up and Faro thrust Vince inside. Then he retrieved the pathetic slippers and put them hastily out of sight in his greatcoat pocket.

But Vince had seen nothing. He lay back, his eyes closed, his face with its bruised black shadows the face of death itself.

Faro shuddered. There would be a reckoning for this night's work. That was for sure.

Somehow he got Vince upstairs and out of his wet clothes, while he forced several drams down his throat. Mrs McGonagall, alerted that they had tried to rescue a suicide, without thankfully having to be told the grim facts, had warming pans in their beds.

Her husband stood watching, his clichés and profundities on the tragedy falling on deaf ears.

Faro took a sleeping draught from Vince's bag and, hoping for the best, administered it full strength. Once he was breathing deeply, Faro retired to his own room.

Removing his greatcoat, he took out Rachel's slippers and laid them reverently side by side on the windowsill. From his other pocket he removed her reticule. Strangely heavy, it contained only one object, that both surprised and alarmed him. A large flat stone.

Suddenly all thoughts of sleep had vanished. Astonished that he could be so detached and think so incisively at this time of grief for Vince, Faro felt almost guilty in his clinical recapitulation of Rachel Deane's death plunge.

As he reconstructed those last minutes in exact detail, remembering how tragically small and vulnerable this poor mad girl had seemed, he sought an answer to the enigma of her sad possessions.

And for some time he sat still, weighing them in his hands as if in some vain hope they might yield a meaning of deeper significance than a madwoman's whim.

118

Chapter Thirteen

After a night of horrendous dreams of which awakening reality was worst of all, Faro overslept that morning.

It was ten o'clock and he had decided against breakfast when Mrs McGonagall announced that he had a caller.

'He's waiting for you outside. In his carriage.' She sounded impressed.

Faro drew aside the lace curtain. The carriage bore what looked like the Deane crest. Tiptoeing into Vince's bedroom he saw that his stepson still slept.

'Let him sleep, Mrs McGonagall. If he should awaken tell him only that I had to go out and will be back soon.'

Wilfred Deane opened the carriage door. Greeted with a sympathetic glance, Faro decided that Deane also looked the worse for a sleepless night, tired and older than his thirty years, with all of his debonair self-confidence vanquished.

'Would you be so good as to spare me a few moments, Inspector Faro – I believe that is how we properly address you,' he added with a wry smile.

'That is so.'

'If you would care to accompany me to Deane Hall? And of course your stepson too, if he wishes.' Gazing across at the house from which Faro had emerged, he shook his head. 'What we have to discuss touches him most nearly. I am almost afraid to enquire as to his condition.'

'He was asleep when I left. I gave him a sleeping draught last night, it seemed the best thing to do—'

'Indeed, in the circumstances that was a wise decision.' As the carriage moved off, he leaned back against the fine leather upholstery. 'I realise this is a very early call. Perhaps you have not yet had time to breakfast,' he added tactfully with an understanding glance at Faro's unshaven face.

Rubbing his chin, Faro smiled: 'I am afraid I had little inclination towards food this morning.'

That sidelong glance of understanding made them allies. 'I have left instructions with the servants that we will partake of breakfast together while we talk.' A sudden dazzling smile brought a measure of charm. 'My valet is at your service too, if you wish to freshen up.'

Remembering the chaotic stunned effects of sudden bereavement in normal homes, Faro expected to see some evidence of deep mourning and was somewhat taken aback to find none.

On the surface Deane Hall's normal activities were quite unruffled and Wilfred Deane's excellent valet performed the function of barber with smooth aplomb. The man made no reference to the house's young mistress having tragically died a few hours before and betrayed not the least curiosity as to Faro's presence at breakfast. It was almost, thought Faro, as if he were well used to the needs of his master's visitors.

Feeling considerably refreshed Faro went down the long staircase and into a panelled dining room bearing a forest of disembodied stags' heads on the walls.

Warming his hands before a welcoming fire, Faro indulged in some mental measurements and decided that this room might have cheerfully accommodated the whole of 9 Sheridan Place.

Wilfred Deane entered and indicated the seat opposite. 'Eat now, Inspector. We will talk later. We will both feel considerably better then, I hope.'

Instead of the humble porridge upon which Faro normally broke his fast, the huge sideboard displayed silver chafing-dishes bearing bacon, eggs, kidneys, sausages and two kinds of fish, kippers and kedgeree.

Taking a modest helping Faro wished that he had more of an appetite. Wilfred Deane, he observed, was not in the least put off his food by the night's terrible events.

Apart from the obligatory mourning touches in Wilfred's attire, always readily at hand in large and affluent houses, there was no indication that he had lost the girl he loved and had hoped to marry.

As they set aside their plates and Faro refused a third cup of tea, Deane's gesture dismissed the hovering table-maids.

'I hope you feel a little restored now, Inspector.'

'I do indeed.'

'Good.' Pausing, Deane tapped his fingers lightly on the table in the manner of one who is giving careful consideration to what he is about to say.

'I owe you an apology for last night, Inspector. My behaviour was quite abominable—'

'You were not in the least impolite – to me.'

'I was to your stepson. And considering all he had been through. Being – being there when it happened. I must have seemed damnably callous.'

'Shock can bring out the worst in all of us, sir.'

Deane sighed. 'I hope some day he will forget my dreadful words. Unfortunately they are true. I spoke truth when I said that we had something in common – that I too loved Rachel. I would have done anything – anything for her. But there was one thing no one could do, no amount of devotion could cure. Her poor sick mind.'

He paused deep in thought. 'I would even have married her, you know. Not to live with her as man and wife, but as her friend and companion. Someone to take care of her during her fits of instability.'

They were interrupted by the sound of slow footsteps and the door opened to admit a tall man with a patriarchal

121

beard. This was the head of the family, Sir Arnold Deane, still recognisable as the man who had been the charisma and life blood of Deane Enterprises.

Faro observed that unlike Wilfred Deane's, Sir Arnold's mourning went further than the clothes he wore. Here was the countenance one would expect to see in such dire circumstances, ashen, bewildered by grief.

'Heard you had a visitor, Wilf.' Although he leaned heavily on a stick, there was nothing lacking in his strong grip as they were introduced. By the intensity of his gaze, Faro realised that here was a man, like himself, who had the extraordinary and often life-preserving gift of summing up friend or foe in thirty seconds.

'Are you sure you are well enough, sir—' Wilfred Deane began.

'Well enough, young fellow. What's that got to do with it, may I ask? How can I be well enough? I've lost my only lass.' He sat down heavily and stared across at Faro, silent for a moment. Turning his head sharply in Deane's direction, he said, 'You've told him about her – her trouble?'

'Yes, sir.'

Sir Arnold sighed. 'Sorry your stepson had to be involved in our problems. He's a fine young chap and an excellent doctor. He'll go a long way but—' he paused and shook his head, 'some day, you, sir, and your lad, may thank heaven that he did not marry her.'

Letting the words sink in, the old man continued: 'Wilf here tells me that when Dr Laurie called at the house she did not even recognise him. You were with him?'

'I was.'

'Very distressing, very distressing. But this peculiarity in her behaviour was not unknown to us. Even in her own family circle, there were days when she pretended she did not know us and that we were strangers to her. Is that not so, Wilf?'

'It is indeed, sir.' And to Faro: 'It was like some vicious little game of let's pretend, or as if her mind was split in two.'

Wilfred Deane looked searchingly at Faro. 'I assume there is a certain amount of trust tantamount with your profession, sir, and what we are telling you is in the strictest confidence. In the past we have tried, and mostly succeeded, to keep Rachel's condition from becoming public knowledge. Pride in the family name—'

'Pride be damned,' Sir Arnold interrupted. 'If pride were all. You forget, I loved the lass. She was all I had left –' and Faro saw how Wilfred winced as the old man added, 'after my David died.'

Sir Arnold's only son had died in a riding accident when Rachel was a child. Was the old man about to mention the strange coincidence that the girl's mother had also committed suicide by drowning? But sighing heavily, he added:

'There is another perhaps more pressing reason for silence. It would also have a very adverse effect on our shareholders' confidence if they thought there was some – well, instability, in the firm who had contracted to build a two-mile-long bridge.'

So that was it, thought Faro. That was the reason, the financial stability as well as respectability. Two good reasons for silence. With commerce possibly the more urgent.

'I realise that Dr Laurie was probably speaking the truth about their assignation. Rachel was missing for a day or two. Slipped out of the house. It was not the first time, was it, Wilf?'

Deane nodded. 'Indeed it was not. When she came home or more often was found and forcibly returned, she relished the secret of where she had been, with a childlike delight in keeping us in the dark.'

'Fortunately we mostly knew where to find her.' Sir Arnold smiled tenderly at the memory. 'With her old nurse in Errol. There was no need for concern on those occasions.'

123

'As far as we know, sir, or were able to find out,' contributed Wilfred.

A heavy silence followed as this information was left to settle with Faro.

'It would have been a great help to my stepson,' he said, 'if you had taken him aside and explained some of what you have told me.'

'I realise that now, and if we had had the slightest idea that—'

Sir Arnold, suddenly overcome, stood up, seized his stick and said: 'I cannot bear this. I am ill. You must excuse me.' He looked dazed, shocked as if realisation had just dawned.

Wilfred Deane touched the bellpull and the butler appeared. 'Sir Arnold will return to his room now.'

The old man brushed aside Faro's outstretched hand and stumbled from the room, dashing the tears from his eyes. They could hear him sobbing aloud as the door closed.

For a moment the two men stared at each other, unable to find the right words. When the sound of footsteps faded Deane continued:

'I realise we should have warned your stepson. Believe me, we would have told him. But how were we to know that he was to be trusted? He might –' He shrugged. 'He might have decided to make some capital out of it.'

'Blackmail, is that what you mean?' demanded Faro sharply.

'Indeed. It has been tried before,' said Wilfred softly. 'There have been other young men. We managed to keep it from Sir Arnold but Rachel was eager for romance and adventure. There was constant danger that she would take up with anyone – and I mean any man,' he stressed the words significantly, 'just for a passing whim.'

Suddenly he put his hands over his eyes. 'Dear God, we should have had her committed. But we couldn't face that, the thought of having her a prisoner for the rest of her life in one of those awful bedlams.'

And Faro found himself recalling Superintendent Johnston's words, that even in the most talented families who produce financial wizards, fate has its little joke and allows genius to spawn the occasional simpleton.

'We tried to do the best we could. This is a large house and we could keep her safe with us, with so little evidence of restraint that I doubt whether even the servants were aware of what was going on. And in those often long sane times, when she was sweet and loving, we foolishly thought that the demons inside her were quelled for ever. She was very clever, you know, and even in her darkest days she could show diabolical cunning. She could outwit us all.'

Wilfred leaned back in his chair. 'And now it's all over. I wish I could say thank God she's at rest. But I can't and I never will.'

There seemed nothing more to say and as Faro stood up to leave, Deane said: 'There will be a funeral, by the way, next Thursday. A small private family affair. If you wish to come – and of course, Dr Laurie.'

'Alas, I am afraid my return to Edinburgh is imminent. I have pressing matters awaiting me there.'

'I quite understand. Nevertheless, if Dr Laurie wishes to be present – at the graveside, there will be no attempt to prevent him so doing. And if he wishes to pay his last respects at the house here, we can promise him our sympathy and understanding.'

As they shook hands he added: 'Will you please convey my sympathy to your stepson. We are both in the same boat, alas, we have both to recover from a broken heart, if you believe such a condition exists.'

And opening the front door: 'There is one more thing, but it may be of some comfort to Dr Laurie. Tell him, as far as Deane's is concerned, that his post with us is secure. There is no question whatever of his being dismissed. We are happy to retain his services as our resident doctor.'

Faro left Dundee hoping only that this was the end of Vince's unfortunate love affair. But in that, as in all else concerned with the events of the past few days, he was mistaken and Vince's involvement with Rachel Deane was to have far-reaching and terrible consequences for all of them.

Chapter Fourteen

In the days that followed Faro could not rid himself of the guilty feeling that he had abandoned Vince at his most vulnerable. Although his sympathetic breakfast with Wilfred at Deane Hall and Sir Arnold's magnanimous attitude towards his young doctor made nonsense of such notions, the certainty that Vince was in mortal danger persisted.

His return to Edinburgh was marked by the anticipation of bad news. None came, only a letter from Vince apologising for the delay in writing. He had been very busy and there had been yet another fatal accident on the bridge:

> The watchman who tried to help us must have missed his footing on the ladder during one of his late-night inspections. He was not discovered until next morning. I cannot begin to tell you how this sad event, recalling as it did so vividly all that is still personally so unbearably painful, has upset me.

Faro felt a shudder of dread, wondering if Vince had also absorbed the more sinister implications of the watchman's death. Besides Faro and Vince, he had been the sole witness of Rachel's suicide. The hand of coincidence seemed once more to have been seriously overplayed.

As he wrestled with another of Edinburgh's sordid domestic crimes, Faro's thoughts turned constantly to

Dundee and the notes he had made on Polly Briggs' suicide and the apparently unconnected death of Hamish McGowan.

Once again he took up *The Scotsman's* report on the tragic death of Rachel Deane:

> Miss Deane took a lively interest in anything connected with Deane Enterprises. Of particular interest to her was the progress being made in the building of the railway bridge and she often dropped in on the bridgeworks to utter words of encouragement to the workers and have a lively chat with her grandfather's engineers.

Faro was impressed by the reporter's active imagination that had completely missed the irony of an evening visit when work had ceased. On this melancholy occasion, Miss Deane had not only dropped in but had also dropped off the bridgeworks to her death.

To Faro, the lies that had been told, white enough to protect the firm and soothe its shareholders, were so transparent he was astounded that intelligent minds could let them go unquestioned. Was this then the hidden tyranny of Deane's, the ability to buy or enforce silence?

Like a festering sore, the incongruities of the events he had witnessed in Dundee grew deeper, stronger in his mind. Many years of training to observe and deduce from given facts could not by swamped by face-saving lies, especially when he had been there, a witness.

And so it was, as the weeks turned into months, that he still found himself on the threshold of sleep reliving those last horrific moments of Rachel Deane's life. In vain he tried to console himself that the girl was mentally unsound, as Wilfred and Sir Arnold had stressed. For only such a sorry fact could justify her mad dash to her death to escape her erstwhile lover and his stepfather.

Faro reconstructed again and again those horrendous scenes, trying to find some grain of sense in Rachel's irrational behaviour. Had she seen Vince and himself in some distorted mirror of her imagination as pursuers? Pursuers who meant to recapture and return her to her imprisonment in Deane Hall. Had her poor sick mind indicated that no one would have the courage to follow her on to the bridge?

Two questions for which Faro would have given much to have answers he believed now must remain for ever unresolved. Did Rachel lose her balance and fall or did she voluntarily decide to quit this life by leaping to her death?

Although Faro now realised that this was one of the conditions of her mental disorder, he would have given much to walk about inside Rachel Deane's mind and discover when Vince's rôle as lover and intended husband of her lucid moments changed into that of mortal enemy.

Did that satisfactorily explain why she had so viciously attacked Vince after asking him to meet her at Magdalen Green? Why she had rushed out of Deane Hall without changing her footwear into something more adequate for heavy rain?

Again and again he saw Vince's pathetic attempts to replace those frail slippers on her feet when he tried to revive her, to warm life into her still body.

But most disturbing of all was the presence of a large round stone in her reticule – and nothing else. Did this indicate a desperate notion that it would help her to sink to the bottom of the river? If so, this clearly implied she had premeditated suicide before leaving Deane Hall. In that case why had she dropped it beside the discarded slippers?

Faro could not get rid of the alternative notion. That the stone had been intended for a more sinister rôle, as a weapon of self-defence should any attempt be made to divert her from her deadly purpose.

And he shuddered with dread, when he realised how fatally effective it could have been, aimed at a pursuer.

Namely Vince, coming up the ladder directly behind her.

Another picture recurred and remained poised, solid and unshakeable.

As the boats searched those dark waters, suddenly illuminated in the flares, the figures of two workmen in overalls inspecting the place from which Rachel had fallen to her death.

One was tall, well-built, the other smaller, more like the night-watchman in build. Their instinct of shielding their faces was natural, but it seemed in retrospect that they stepped back hurriedly, guiltily, as if agitated at being observed or recognised.

What were they doing there? Were they taking their work seriously, hurriedly repairing or replacing some evidence of neglect or malfunction that might have caused Rachel's death?

Another thought crept in. Had they been her executioners? Had a trap been sprung to make it look like suicide?

After another dawn of birdsong which defeated his attempts to continue sleeping or make sense of the notes sprawled about the bed, Faro realised he was getting nowhere. One pointer remained: since the tone of her note to Vince indicated that their meeting was to be secret, it seemed hardly likely that Rachel had advertised her intentions of going to the bridge at Deane Hall.

It followed that if no one had known of her purpose and no one could have foreseen that her flight would take her to the bridge, how then could that fatal trap have been sprung?

Unless she had confided in someone in Deane Hall.

Faro sighed wearily. That didn't make sense but still the picture of the two men in overalls refused to be banished.

Remaining uneasy, anxious on Vince's behalf without ever quite knowing why, he was relieved as well

as delighted to receive a letter informing him to expect
his stepson home on a brief visit:

> My old friend Dr Sam has recently taken up a post
> as assistant to the police pathologist and is getting
> married. I am to attend the wedding. You will be
> interested to learn that since I last wrote you the
> McG. have had word from the missing Kathleen.
> She did not care for London and is now working in a
> milliner's shop in Rose Street (yes, Edinburgh). The
> McG. are jubilant at the news and plans are afoot to
> visit her. I have promised to find time to call in and
> pay their compliments . . .

Going downstairs to the kitchen to give Mrs Brook the
glad tidings, Faro was relieved to know that there was now
a happy ending to what seemed like the ominous disappearance of the two young women. Charlie McGowan's
widow had returned for her father-in-law's funeral with
a perfectly logical reason for her absence. Now Kathleen
Neil was safe and sound in Edinburgh.

Faro remembered having decided many years ago that
suspicions without foundation were chronic and incurable
diseases of the detective's imagination. But he had also
discovered in twenty years with the Edinburgh City Police
that, left alone, time often provides simple explanations
for the darkest and most baffling mysteries.

Perhaps it was mere curiosity that directed him towards
Rose Street as the shops were putting on their shutters.
As he stared into a milliner's shop window, he observed
a pretty fair-haired young woman arranging bonnets.

This must be 'the fair Kathleen' and on impulse he
opened the door, bravely determined not to be overwhelmed by such an entirely feminine establishment.

To his enquiry, the girl shook her head. 'I wish I
was Miss Neil,' she said wistfully. 'I only work for her.'

Disappointed, Faro left with the distinct impression
that Kathleen Neil must have her own private reasons
for concealing from the McGonagalls that her position

131

was grander and more affluent than she had led them to believe.

Faro now awaited his stepson's arrival with pleasure not untinged with misgivings. Remembering the shattered condition in which they had parted company, he was not quite sure what to expect. Although confident that one day Vince armed with the natural resilience of youth would pick up some of the pieces of his life, Faro would not have speculated with certainty that he could also put them together again.

Remembering how long it had taken him to sort out his own life when Lizzie died, he expected Vince to be inevitably changed by the bitter experience of loss.

On the surface, he was relieved to see that his fears and gnawing anxieties were groundless. Here was the cheerful, well-balanced young man, his impish sense of humour undiminished.

Only in sudden silences, a sentence left unfinished, did the cracks below the surface reveal themselves and a sudden bleakness in his eyes showed that Vince's mind had drifted again to that sad shore where he had lost his Rachel Deane.

It was not, however, until they sat at supper together that Vince drained his glass of claret and sighed heavily: 'Well, Stepfather, how long does it take to recover, would you say? I cannot forget her, you know. I see her everywhere.

'The Deanes have been unfailingly kind and considerate. I was wrong about them, I know that now. They were trying to protect poor Rachel from herself. Wilfred was very decent to me at the funeral and asked me to dine with them at Deane Hall. He told me much the same story as I understand he told you. And Sir Arnold too.'

With a sad smile he added: 'Seems that my services as doctor are well thought of, at least. Although I had behaved so outrageously, they were prepared to forget the past. All very heartening, Stepfather, especially as

132

they have seen fit to accompany their goodwill towards me with a substantial rise in salary.

'I was very touched when the old man said there was no one they would rather have seen Rachel marry, as he thought very highly of me both as a doctor and as a young man with excellent qualities.'

He darted a look at Faro. 'Are you pleased? I was.' And without waiting for an answer: 'I am now a constant visitor to Deane Hall, free to use the library too. You would love that. Once a week I go and examine Sir Arnold, listen to his heart and that sort of thing. Then afterwards I have dinner with Wilfred and a game of billiards or a hand at cards. Who would have thought it?'

Who indeed, wondered Faro somewhat cynically, feeling uncharitable for his newly aroused suspicions that Vince too might have been bought by Deane's. Hiding his thoughts, he merely smiled, remarking that he had recently encountered Wilfred Deane on Princes Street on his way to a business meeting.

'Yes, I gather he comes fairly often, so he has very good reasons for wishing that accursed bridge was complete.'

'So he said.'

'He didn't mention me?' Vince asked.

'We were both in a hurry, we only had time to exchange the civilities.'

Faro would not easily forget his reaction to recognising Deane emerging from a carriage outside the Royal British Hotel. That familiar figure jolted him back to their last unhappy meeting and wishing heartily that this encounter could be avoided, he realised that this was impossible. Since one had to step aside to allow the other passage, a lack of acknowledgement would have amounted to rudeness.

It had to be said for Deane that Faro saw in his fleeting expression of annoyance and even embarrassment, an equal eagerness to avoid this meeting. But the politenesses had to be observed.

133

Both men bowed, raised their hats, wished each other good day, enquired earnestly about each other's health and agreed that the weather was abominable.

Deane went further. He felt obliged to explain: 'I am here for a meeting with our Edinburgh shareholders. More frequently than I would wish with that infernally tedious train journey in both directions.'

But each saw in the other's face how even indirect reference to the unfinished Tay Bridge touched unpleasant memories. And it was with considerable relief that they bowed and parted once more.

Vince sighed. 'The fact that we both loved Rachel is a bond between us. It keeps her alive for us.' His eyes suddenly filled and he shook his head. 'I'm not in any danger of ever forgetting her. As I told you, I see her everywhere. At first – after the funeral, I was in a daze, those early days.

'Can you imagine, I used to follow perfectly innocent young ladies in the Overgait, terrified them by my approaches. I just wanted to speak to them, be comforted, if you like, because there was something, the way they walked, or the set of a bonnet, a laugh or a cloud of dark hair that reminded me of Rachel. Even such glimpses were oddly consoling. I can see now that I was always searching – and will continue to do so, alas, for that lost happiness.'

He shrugged apologetically. 'I know this isn't making sense, Stepfather.'

It was Faro's turn to be sympathetic. He knew all about such reactions as a phenomenon of loss, and had entertained a persistent belief that Lizzie must still be alive somewhere if he could only find her again.

'After your dear mother died, lad, I found myself looking for her in shops, walking down the High Street, haunting crowded places, staring into strangers' faces, just longing to see someone who reminded me of her so that I might relive a tiny fragment of our life together.

'That's it exactly. I thought I was going mad.' Vince

sounded relieved. 'Does the search ever end, I wonder? At the moment, I imagine going on to the end of my days trying to find someone exactly like her and yet knowing deep down that I never will.'

They were interrupted by Mrs Brook's arrival to draw the curtains and attend to the fire. When she departed Vince told him about the wedding at St Giles and added: 'There is something I have promised McGonagall. I must find time for this.'

He took from his pocket a brooch in a velvet case. 'This belonged to his grandmother who was Kathleen's great-aunt.'

The brooch was of diamond and pearl in the shape of a shamrock. 'I suspect it's been the lifeline of the McGonagalls, in and out of pawn, but things are looking up now and he wants Kathleen to have it. Says it will bring her luck. Have you seen the shop, by the way?'

'Aye, and very smart it is too. Prosperous. She should do well in there.'

When next day Vince returned from visiting the Rose Street shop Faro was very glad he had kept his suspicions about Kathleen's modest establishment to himself. His stepson, at least, was oblivious to any interesting possibilities as to how she might have suddenly acquired a thriving millinery business.

Faro wondered if in fact Vince was aware that Kathleen was the owner not the employee when his thoughts were diverted by a happy glow long absent from Vince's countenance.

'I must say, Stepfather, that she is quite a stunner. I was quite captivated. I'm only sorry we did not meet earlier, when she was in Dundee,' he added ruefully.

And Faro that night felt more cheerful than had been the case for many a day, for Vince could talk of nothing but the fair Kathleen.

'I should have liked to have taken her to the wedding. I fancy she would have enjoyed that. She would have been a sensation in one of her delicious bonnets too. Oh, incidentally, there was one familiar face. Remember Dr Ramsey?'

'I do indeed. The dour young police surgeon at Dundee.'

'The same. He was Sam's best man. Seems they are cousins. And let me tell you, away from those doleful surroundings, he is anything but dour, quite the contrary.

'As for the fair Kathleen, I haven't much time now but I'm hoping to be better organised when next I come home for a weekend. And, of course, there is always the possibility of her visiting Paton's Lane to see the McGonagalls. She did mention that.'

Faro was intrigued. 'I should very much like to meet her.'

'And so you shall, Stepfather. I thought we might have luncheon at the Café Royal before I leave.'

Faro had a table near the window and as the couple approached and he shook hands with Kathleen he suppressed a smile. His first impression was that Vince had in fact succeeded in his search. Whether consciously or not, he had found a girl who reminded him of his lost love.

True, on closer acquaintance he realised that any resemblance to Rachel Deane, whom he had met so briefly and under somewhat trying circumstances, was quite superficial. And during the meal it faded completely as he studied this pretty girl, so shy and overwhelmed by her surroundings that they had the effect of rendering her almost inarticulate.

When later he mentioned those first impressions, Vince shook his head firmly. 'They are not in the least alike, Stepfather. But I do know what you mean. Perhaps that's what attracted me to her when we first met. I can't explain it, except that they are basically the same type, rather than anything more definite.

'I had only seen her photograph at Willie McGonagall's and that was taken when she was very young. She's much prettier now.'

A now buoyant Vince departed for Dundee, leaving his stepfather gratified by promises of fairly regular visits home in future, for which Vince was even prepared to endure cheerfully that abominable train journey. To be near his new love, thought Faro, seeing through any other excuses Vince had readily available.

And so the day came when Vince threw casually into the conversation that he was seriously considering the possibility of a situation in Edinburgh again.

As Faro suspected, the fair Kathleen was the main reason.

'Who knows, Stepfather, perhaps in the not too distant future I may be able to achieve the circumstances which would allow me the right credentials to set up successfully as a family doctor,' he added with a shy smile.

'Are congratulations in order?' Faro asked, his first feeling of delight mingled with gratitude that Vince was making a spectacular recovery from his tragic infatuation for Rachel Deane.

Chapter Fifteen

To Faro's question regarding his intentions, Vince grinned sheepishly. 'A bit early for that, Stepfather. But I have hopes. I mean, Kathleen is always glad to see me, never refuses an invitation. And of course, the McGonagalls would be delighted.'

'Scarcely a valid reason for choosing a wife, is it, lad?'

'I know that perfectly well, Stepfather. I haven't asked the lady formally but her attitude has given me every reason to believe she will accept me.'

Observing Faro's veiled glance, he added hastily: 'No, no, Stepfather. Nothing like that. No unbridled passion this time. This is quite a different courtship, if that's what I might call it. And I'm very glad it is so. All very proper and up to now nothing more has been exchanged between us than a chaste goodnight kiss – on the cheek. But,' he added cheerfully, 'sometimes I suspect – and hope, dammit – that my chaste fair Kathleen has hidden fires.'

Faro received this information on the progress of Vince's courtship with mixed feelings. Did the cautious reserve on Kathleen's side involve the ownership of the milliner's shop and confirm his own suspicions regarding the possibility of a protector, a secret lover?

Vince was smiling happily. 'I'm glad that there has been this restraint between us. It has given me time to sort out my own feelings. I shouldn't like Kathleen to discover – or even to imagine for one moment – that she was my second choice.'

'Does she know about Rachel?'

Vince shook his head. 'I didn't consider that was necessary.'

The likelihood that he himself was a second choice had not occurred to Vince's unsuspicious nature. Direct and honest in his dealings, if he had a fault it was to believe that as he always spoke truth, then so too did others.

'I shall certainly tell her, if she consents to be my wife. That would only be proper.'

'I detect a certain reluctance. Are you afraid that your unhappy love affair might influence her?'

'At this stage, perhaps I am.' And with a heartfelt sigh, 'Let's face it, Stepfather, I can now see quite clearly that whatever my feelings about Rachel and hers about me, marriage between us would have been a complete disaster. Her fits of unreason – insanity, let's give it an honest name – were going to get worse.'

He paused and then added, 'The heightened emotions and physical demands of married life would have increased her instability. In such cases the bearing of children is a further hazard, quite capable of throwing the young mother over the edge.

'This is not conjecture on my part, it is alas a proven medical fact, and something not at all infrequent in unbalanced young women. Paul Ramsey, my new friend, lent me a very interesting book on the subject just last week.'

Was this all Vince needed to prove to himself that he had loved not wisely but too well, thought Faro cynically?

'There would have been little in the way of family life for us and a sad bleak prospect for any children we might have brought into the world. We would have been wise to make the decision to remain childless and I know now that willing as I was to marry her, eager for her to be my wife, my rôle would have been increasingly that of attendant doctor rather than husband.'

As Vince left for Dundee, Faro said: 'Let me know

in time when you are coming again and I'll drop in a note inviting Kathleen to dinner.'

'What a splendid idea.'

From Faro's point of view, hoping for a glimpse of Kathleen's hidden fires, that evening two weeks later was unremarkable and even, for him, a little boring.

Kathleen again seemed overwhelmed by her surroundings and spent a lot of time gazing around her and admiring the furniture. Otherwise he found her once again more inarticulate than he thought accountable from shyness and a certain awe of Vince's famous stepfather.

Reserved and retiring in company, with little to say for herself, Kathleen was also, Faro reminded himself, the shrewd business woman, whether as manager or owner of the Rose Street establishment.

That second meeting also confirmed her lack of sexual attraction. He realised from his limited experience that apparently shy women are capable of stripping off a colourless personality with their garments once the bedroom door is closed. But in Kathleen's case, the idea of her being anyone's secret mistress became increasingly absurd as the evening dragged to its weary close.

Only once did he succeed in raising her animation. In the drawing room was a grand piano belonging to the previous owner of the house, which Faro had acquired with other furniture. Apart from his daughters' visits when they taxed its grandeur with scales and pianoforte exercises, it remained untouched.

Observing that on several occasions Kathleen's wistful glance had strayed towards it, he asked in sudden hope: 'Do you play?'

She shrugged. 'A little and not well.'

'Mr McGonagall mentioned that you sang very sweetly and were very talented,' Faro said encouragingly.

She laughed. 'He told you about my "Song of the Forest", did he?'

'Your bird calls?'

'Yes.'

Vince beamed. 'I say, Kathleen, won't you give us a rendering?'

She looked at Faro for approval, but when he added his plea, she shrank back in her chair: 'Oh no, I don't think – really—'

Vince stood up, took her firmly by the arm. 'Come along, Kathleen. No use hiding your talent under a bushel. Now it's your turn to sing for your supper.'

She played a few chords hesitantly and then gathering courage, suddenly lost her shyness and trilled happily through the blackbird's call, the laverock and the nightingale and an assortment of wild birds, ending with the humble robin's song.

Faro and Vince applauded, their response instinctive. It was really quite remarkable. McGonagall had been right. Here was a girl with an astonishing gift.

As she closed the piano lid, Faro said: 'You could have made a very good career for yourself on the stage.'

Kathleen shook her head. 'I have little ability as an actress and I have been a great disappointment to poor Uncle Willie. He despaired of me when I couldn't learn all those long speeches in Shakespeare. I was always more at home with wardrobe, making costumes. That was how I first became interested in creating my own millinery.'

And that, as far as Faro was concerned, was her longest speech of the evening. Having bowed over her hand, as Vince escorted her back home to Rose Street, he closed the front door thoughtfully.

Vince, he decided, had exchanged the enigma of Rachel Deane for the enigma of Kathleen Neil with her downcast eyes, modest glances, and long silences.

Faro was disappointed. Oh dear, dear, this was not at all the wife he had hoped Vince would choose. He had always envisaged his stepson with a young woman of spirit, his intellectual equal, one who would respond to and enhance the camaraderie between the two men with her own wit.

Ideally, he realised, he was hoping for a stepdaughter-in-law who would grow as close to him as Vince. Now

141

he recognised sadly that he was hoping for the impossible. Did such a girl even exist beyond the realms of fantasy?

Well, since his Lizzie died, he had but once thought he had encountered such a perfect woman.

And deliberately he thrust those sad thoughts aside.

To more practical matters, he knew that once the engagement was announced and the wedding date fixed, he had best set about moving out of Sheridan Place and finding himself another home.

He smiled suddenly, realising he was back at precisely that same hurdle where he had been four months earlier, when Vince had written to tell him of his forthcoming marriage. During the interval between Rachel's death and his decision to propose to Kathleen Neil, while summer had bloomed and faded into golden autumn, time had also gone about its business dulling the pain in the human heart.

So much had changed since then. Only on Tay Bridge, it seemed that little progress had been made. Passengers from both cities who had anticipated an easier journey between Edinburgh and Dundee grumbled more than ever and with reason. Older folk wondered whether they would live long enough to see it finished.

Stage comics made jokes about it. And pithy sayings were springing up, parodies of Robert Burns:

> My love is like a red, red rose . . .
> And I shall love you, dear, always,
> Till the first train steams over the Tay Bridge.

If Vince's courtship of Kathleen Neil gave Faro cause for concern, then he was also delighted that Vince had made new friendships in Dundee, with the young police surgeon Dr Ramsey and, more surprisingly, with Wilfred Deane. On several occasions the two had travelled to Edinburgh together in Deane's carriage, a welcome relief to the abominable train journey.

Faro chided himself on his own base ingratitude. Vince

could hardly be blamed for choosing a wife who did not meet his stepfather's requirements. Kathleen Neil might be somewhat lack-lustre, but she had been capable of repairing the damage and reconstructing some happiness from those sad ashes of Vince's first love.

At first, Faro had regarded the entry of Kathleen into their lives as perhaps holding some vital clue to Polly Briggs' disappearance and subsequent death. But Kathleen was vague on the subject of Polly except to say that she didn't know where she went after they parted in London. Her refusal to be drawn into any discussion amounted, Faro thought, to almost callous indifference to her friend's fate which in any other person than Kathleen Neil, might have aroused his suspicions that she was involved in Polly's demise.

He had long prided himself on being a shrewd assessor of character but as he failed completely to get beyond those mouse-like qualities of timidity and shyness, Kathleen did not strike him as being capable of calculated murder.

The further explanation was simpler. The friendship which Jean McGonagall had described 'so close, like sisters' but which Briggs had described as 'a bad influence' had been on Polly's side rather than Kathleen's.

And Polly Briggs must remain an enigma, while the mysterious circumstances of her death were strictly the concern of the Dundee City Police. Faro still had hopes of learning the truth some day. In the words of Voltaire he was fond of quoting: 'Love and murder will out.'

They did not fail him now.

On one of his visits home, Vince told him that Dr Ramsey, in his cups, had confided certain disturbing medical facts about his post-mortem on Polly Briggs.

'Paul is certain that she didn't take her own life and that she was already dead before she was put into the water.'

'What are you suggesting?'

'Drowning, as you know, Stepfather, is death by

143

asphyxia, caused by air being prevented from reaching the lungs. Whether or not suicide is intended, the body instinctively reacts with an initial struggle during which water is gulped into the lungs. Eventually they become waterlogged and this weighs the body down enough for it to sink. The unmistakable sign we look for is a fine froth in the mouth and nostrils but the main internal indication is a ballooning of the lungs as a result of distension with water.'

Vince paused dramatically. 'Paul has been seriously concerned about his findings.'

'Which were?' Faro demanded.

'The signs of death by drowning were absent. There was every indication that the girl had been dead for several hours and rigor had already set in before the corpse was disposed of by throwing it into the water. Paul's further examination revealed a contusion at the base of the skull, not immediately obvious because of her thick hair, but this he firmly regarded as being the fatal blow.'

'And what were his conclusions?'

'In his opinion the girl did not drown. She was murdered.'

'Then why in God's name hasn't he done something about it before now?'

'He did. All that he told me, and I believe him, was written in his report. He left it on his desk in readiness to send to the Procurator Fiscal. Then, in the middle of the night, two men arrived at his lodgings. There had been an accident, would he come quickly.

'When he got outside they bundled him into a cab, beat him up and advised him if he wanted his family to stay healthy and his career likewise, then he had better accept that Polly Briggs committed suicide.'

'Naturally, he did as he was told,' said Faro contemptuously.

'Naturally. Not all men are brave, Stepfather. Some value a future and a peaceful life. He has a wife and two

144

young children. And now not only are they in danger, but also if at this late date he reveals all to Superintendent Johnston, he will no doubt lose his position as police surgeon.'

'So what has he decided?'

Vince shrugged. 'He is suffering enough, haunted ever since by assisting this miscarriage of justice and several times he has attempted to make a clean breast of it. On that day when we visited the mortuary, soon after he was beaten up, he was absolutely terrified.'

Observing his stepfather's expression, he said: 'I am only telling you because the case of Polly Briggs is beyond your jurisdiction. Otherwise I would have remained silent, respecting Paul's confidence, and I must ask you to do the same.'

'Tell me one more thing, if you please?'

'And what is that?'

'Has your friend any suspicions of the murderer's identity?'

'Oh yes, indeed. He suspects that this was no jealous lover's crime passionel. The fact that his confidential report on the post-mortem was read and action so immediately taken, suggests to him that Polly Briggs' murder is part of a much larger crime, carried out by an organisation so powerful that they have spies in the police department.'

'Deane Enterprises, in fact,' said Faro slowly.

'Possibly.' Vince made the admission reluctantly.

'And how does this affect your friendship with Wilfred Deane?'

'Not at all. Why should it? I doubt whether Wilf has ever heard of Polly Briggs,' he added loyally. 'Besides, Stepfather, there are others who might wish to buy silence. The shareholders of the gentlemen's select clubs, for instance.'

As autumn spread a golden glory of sunsets over Arthur's Seat and leaves fell like drops of blood on the banks of the

River Tay, Faro found his hands full with two particularly brutal murders and a plot to assassinate a royal personage (neither of which have any place in this chronicle).

One day, looking for notes he had made on an earlier case with some similarities, he was searching through a trunk in the attics of Sheridan Place. Once the property of his late father, Constable Magnus Faro, this receptacle had become the last resting place for clues and objects relating to unsolved murders. When he moved from Sheridan Place into a smaller establishment, it would be prudent to discard this detritus of twenty years with the Edinburgh City Police.

As he pushed back the lid, there were the slippers and reticule belonging to Rachel Deane. Long since past any hope that they might conceal some amazing truth that had escaped him, he might as well begin his clearing-out operations by consigning these to Mrs Brook's rubbish bin.

Weighing them in his hands, he wondered why he had retained these mementoes of that distressing event, storing them with this battered collection of clues that had not led anywhere. Was it only a faint hope that one day he might still find an answer? Why had he not got rid of them immediately he unpacked in Edinburgh and discovered them in his luggage?

He had kept them secret too long. He could not produce them now without renewing for Vince the terrible emotions of Rachel's death.

Replacing them, he closed the lid hurriedly. But their presence in the trunk upstairs continued to haunt him, arousing emotions for him too. Emotions of dissatisfaction. Certain of a mystery concerning Rachel's suicide, he felt that somehow he had failed Vince and himself.

In view of Dr Ramsey's confession to Vince, Faro also felt guiltily that he had failed Polly Briggs' father and it was no consolation to tell himself that there was nothing he could do, since Dundee crimes were none of his business.

146

But Faro was not used to failure, it left a bad taste in his mouth. Considering that he had a high success rate with people who meant nothing to him at all, it was very humiliating that results were dismally lacking in a case involving those near and dear to him, particularly his stepson.

He wished he could wipe clean the slate of the nightmare that persisted of the suicide he had witnessed and had been so helpless to prevent. An indelible scene that must for ever link his memory with that short disastrous visit to Dundee.

Chapter Sixteen

Vince's next visit brought news that William McGonagall was to appear in Edinburgh, at an open air production before Her Majesty the Queen in the park adjacent to the Palace of Holyroodhouse.

This was to be a gala variety and an elegant version of the penny gaff circus. Her Majesty was well known to have a surprisingly unsophisticated, even childlike taste in entertainment. And circuses, it seemed, were irresistible to her. She had approved a programme including clowns, a juggler and a magician called Alpha Omega, but clapping her hands with quite unqueenly glee, had asked especially for lions and trapeze artistes.

Her Majesty, it was observed, had a penchant for watching other mortals risking life and limb on the high wire or with wild animals. She had a wistful partiality for brave lion-tamers in leopard-skins. This savage form of amusement did not go unmarked by her courtiers, suggesting as it did wry comparisons with a less tender-hearted, sentimental monarch, the Emperor Nero feeding Christians to the lions in Ancient Rome. Her Majesty's wish granted, the lion act was found and commanded to appear, although no setting was less like the Colosseum than Queeen's Park overlooked by the grandeur of Arthur's Seat, its slopes resplendent in a purple blaze of autumn heather.

On the other hand, all was far from sweetness and light in the Central Office of the Edinburgh City Police, feverishly drafting in extra constables from outlying areas. Faro listened patiently to Superintendent McIntosh's grumbles about the considerable expense involved.

As senior detective, protecting the Queen on twice-yearly visits was Faro's responsibility and constant headache. He could well have done without the hazards involved in mounting this additional event.

The Superintendent smiled grimly. 'Sometimes I think that Her Majesty is either remarkably courageous or lacks imagination.'

Faro, who had only recently foiled an assassination attempt, opted for the latter. 'To Fenians and others with deep-seated grudges, or who are simply mad, we might now add escaped lions.'

The Superintendent gave him a hard look as he continued: 'And wild beasts are also a threat to the lesser mortals of her realm, like all the Edinburgh citizens who will be drawn to this circus to please their children and for a glimpse of royalty, as well as those aforesaid lions.'

McIntosh groaned as Faro pointed to the plan on his desk. 'Let's make no mistake about it, sir, we will need a great many extra safety measures. Measures which you will recall are difficult enough to put into effect when stone walls are involved and massive buildings with guarded entrances.'

After the Queen's recent escape, the idea of her sitting in a frail circus tent in a huge park surrounded by a dense crowd of people, from which a shot could be fired and an assassin make his escape in the confusion, did nothing for Faro's nerves as grimly he supervised elaborate security measures.

These included a specially constructed Royal Box which could be under constant police guard and which had no access from underneath as had the tiers of wooden seats.

It was with some relief that he scrutinised the programme. McGonagall was to recite 'The Battle of Bannockburn', calculated to enhance his credits and boost his further bookings with the information 'As performed before Her Majesty the Queen and the Crowned

149

Heads of Europe', some of that bevy of relatives he hoped would be accompanying her.

Vince, who had heard McGonagall's Bannockburn, expressed doubts about such a choice. 'It just may not kindle the Queen's heart with kindness when she hears the heroic stanzas regarding English King Edward's sorry defeat.'

The McGonagalls duly arrived in Edinburgh and hastened to Kathleen's flat above the milliner's shop. There they would stay for the weekend, Jean having been prevailed upon to leave her little brood to bask in the vicarious glory of her husband's triumphant appearance before royalty.

She whispered that she was hoping – just hoping – that she might be presented and with this in mind, had purchased a new bonnet and cape. New to her that was, for it had cost two and sixpence from one of the ladies in Dundee who sold cast-offs for the wealthy wives of the jute lords in Broughty Ferry.

Faro received all this information from Vince who was to escort Jean and Kathleen on the gala evening. As they proudly took their seats, those special seats of privilege opposite the Royal Box reserved for guests of performers, Jean McGonagall was a happy woman.

Further she confessed to Faro that both she and Willie were delighted since Vince was 'like one of our own now'. It was obvious through the visit that they took every opportunity of beaming fondly upon the couple in the manner of those who believe an announcement of a romantic nature is imminent.

His presence in the guest box necessary in the line of duty, Faro took his seat beside Jean, Kathleen and Vince. As the performance began he was amused to notice that, in common with most of the members of the audience, Jean and Kathleen were more interested in observing the royal party, whose jewels outsparkled the performers' many glittering costumes.

For Faro too, acrobats and clowns took second place as

150

he watched the Royal Box, not from motives of curiosity but of acute anxiety for any unscheduled moves in that direction. Sharp-eyed, constantly alert, his hand never left the pistol in his greatcoat pocket.

The bareback riders, the performing dogs, Alpha Omega's magic went down very well. And then the safety net was placed between the audience and the ring for the entrance of the lions and their tamer.

Safely behind bars but bringing with them the smell of wild animals and an exciting but scaringly alien whiff of the jungle, the lions in their ornate cage arrived behind plumed circus horses, also less than happy at the burden of ferocity they escorted.

Part of the act no doubt, but impressive. The roars were convincing enough to replace smiles with whimpers of fear from the more sensitive children and shivers of tremulous excitement from their elders.

Faro looked across at Her Majesty, clapping her hands enthusiastically as the Great Tonga (born Tony Brown in Coventry) bowed before her. His magnificent frame was only partially covered by a leopard-skin presumably from one of his charges who had refused to obey him.

Muscles rippling, the Great Tonga skirmished playfully with his lions, assisted by a long pole to keep them conveniently respectful. With this light armour he prodded the more sluggish performers who had a tendency to yawn while others leaped up and down on boxes obligingly showing their teeth.

At last came the moment the audience had been waiting for. The animals were shooed into their cage and bundled away by the clowns. One solitary lion remained.

'Absolute silence, if you please,' demanded the ring-master. 'It is essential for the safety of Monsieur Tonga that we have absolute silence. Any sudden noise which might frighten this savage animal could be fatal. I beseech you, ladies and gentlemen—'

After a roll of drums, Tonga opened the lion's mouth and stuck his head inside. Seconds later he withdrew it,

151

patting the lion as if he had no more harm in him than a pussy-cat by the fire.

Faro was near enough to see that he had hardly been in any real danger since the poor beast was toothless, elderly, had mange and was probably fated to die of tranquil old age.

Along with compassion he felt a rising tide of anger. He could not abide zoos, or the sight of wild animals imprisoned. His dislike of caged creatures, animals or birds, was regarded with wry amusement by his colleagues at the Central Office. And why not, since his everyday activities had succeeded in putting so many human male-factors behind bars.

After the lions came McGonagall in borrowed but handsome robes depicting Robert the Bruce in chain mail, with magnificent flowing velvet cloak and a splendid fiery red wig which took several years off his age while adding an agreeable several inches to his stature.

Slowly he emerged from the curtained entrance and in stately slow measure gained the centre spotlight. After bowing to the Queen, he immediately thrust forward his left leg and raised his right hand – more, thought Faro, as if working a pump handle than handling his cardboard sword to any purpose.

Mouth forming a complete circle, round as a cannon's mouth and with the ardour of a warrior who fights for glory, he plunged full tilt into 'The Battle of Bannockburn':

> Sir Robert the Bruce at Bannockburn
> Beat the English in every wheel and turn,
> And made them fly in great dismay
> From the field without delay . . .

Faro lost count of the verses which led to the flight of the English army. It seemed that Her Majesty, now whispering to one of her ladies-in-waiting behind her fan, shared his confusion:

152

. . . King Edward was amazed at the sight,
And he got wounded in the fight:
And he cried, Oh heaven, England's lost, and
   I'm undone,
Alas, alas, where shall I run?
Then he turned his horse, and rode on afar
And never halted till he reached Dunbar.

It was over and McGonagall, acknowledging polite
applause, promptly announced that seeing his little
poem had been so well received he might have the
honour of addressing one to Her Majesty, especially for
herself.

Most August Empress of India, and of Great
   Britain the Queen
I most humbly beg your pardon, hoping you will
   not think it mean
That a poor poet that lives in Dundee
Would be so presumptuous to write this poem unto
   Thee.
Most lovely Empress of India, and England's
   generous Queen,
I Send you an Address, I have written on
   Scotland's Bard,
Hoping that you will accept it, and not be with
   me too hard,
Nor fly into a rage, but be as Kind and Condescending
As to give me your Patronage.
Beautiful Empress of India and England's Gracious
   Queen
And I think if your Majesty likes it, right pleased
   you will be
And my heart it will leap with joy, if it is patronised
   by Thee.
Most Mighty Empress of India, and England's
   beloved Queen,
Most handsome to be seen.

Mild applause, some exchange of amused glances, but not a great deal emanating from the Royal Box, thought Faro sadly. McGonagall had taken a liberty in presuming to address Her Majesty and he doubted whether that would do him any good. Poor Willie was irrepressible, although Faro decided he should stick to acting as he had no great future as a poet.

Now the ring was taken over by more magicians, performing dogs leaping through rings and on and off the horses' backs, clowns tumbling and throwing buckets of water over one another. Some tight-rope walking and trapeze swinging, then the ring-master announced the climax of the evening's entertainment. They were to see a death-defying trapeze act, at the end of which the beautiful Selina would swing above the lion cage and dive into a tank of flames.

The high-wire performance was unremarkable until, after mild applause, the ring-master again begged for absolute silence. A lion's cage, high-sided but roofless, was wheeled in, the safety net dragged away by the clowns, the tank pulled forward and torches thrown in.

Flames leaped high causing the lion to pace his cage with angry frightened roars of protest.

'Poor beast. It's terrified of fire. That shouldn't be allowed,' Faro whispered to Vince.

But his protest fell on deaf ears as all eyes turned to the apex of the tent forty feet above their heads, where the trapeze swung lazily with Selina, a pretty girl in spangled tights, barely visible through the pink smoke.

Back and forward she swung and at the last moment to an accompanying roll of drums she leaped on to the platform and plunged through the smoke above the lion's cage and into the burning tank.

There was a horrified roar from the audience as the crowd surged to their feet. But before panic could break out, a roll of drums, a spotlight on the trapeze high above their heads. There bowing to the crowd was Alpha Omega and the beautiful Selina, with not a singe mark or a whiff of smoke to tarnish her spangles.

A sigh of relief, an outburst of cheering. Then as the brass band played the National Anthem, the audience remained on their feet until the royal party left the box.

Vince and Jean were still applauding while Faro sat rigid in his seat with Kathleen beside him, her hand grasping his arm, her face white with terror.

A strange excitement, like the lifting of a shutter in the photographer's camera, surged through him. As they followed the crowd swarming out of the tent, Jean was asking Vince:

'But how did he do it? Why, we all saw her fall. Have you any idea?'

Faro looked at her. 'Oh yes, I know now how it was done. I should have seen it at once. Fool that I was.'

'Do tell, do tell us.'

Suddenly aware of them again, Faro turned away from the tent. 'It's just a simple magician's trick. I won't spoil the magic for you.'

One of the clowns had come over and was speaking to Kathleen. She seemed to know him and he was being introduced to Jean and Vince.

'I must go. I'm still on duty,' said Faro.

'Join us later, won't you, Stepfather?'

As Faro hurried in the direction of the royal party, now boarding their carriages, he glanced back wondering if Kathleen's establishment also provided wigs for the clowns and costumes for the circus performers.

'Stepfather's very jaunty tonight,' Vince whispered to Kathleen as Jean chatted animatedly to the clown.

Kathleen smiled. 'Isn't he always?'

'I shouldn't be in the least surprised if he spotted a criminal in the crowd. I know that look of his. Like a bloodhound on the trail. Yes, he's definitely on to something.'

Having seen Her Majesty safely restored to Holyroodhouse and his men dismissed, a very relieved Faro walked

155

homeward through the now almost deserted Queen's Park, where the circus tent was already being dismantled.

As he sauntered past, the clown whom he recognised as the one known to Kathleen, hailed him.

'Inspector Faro, isn't it? Thought I recognised you in the front row, sir. You didn't know me, of course.' And as he dragged off wig and false nose, Faro found himself looking into the countenance of Polly Briggs' father whom he had last encountered outside the police mortuary in Dundee.

Briggs brushed aside Faro's congratulations on the evening's performance. There was something else on his mind and Faro guessed that this must concern his dead daughter.

'I see you had that Kathleen with you. She's done very well for herself with that rich man, by the look of things. Was that him with you?'

'No, that was my stepson, Dr Laurie,' said Faro in a tone of annoyance.

'I see,' said Briggs, a mocking smile indicating that he saw all too clearly. 'Jean hinted that there was love in the air.'

Faro found scant comfort in the knowledge that he had been right about Kathleen's rich protector, apparently common knowledge to everyone but his stepson. Shrewd and intelligent in many ways, honest himself, Vince would never be so unchivalrous as to doubt a lady's word or her virtue.

As Briggs continued to regard him with veiled amusement, Faro cursed Jean McGonagall. 'The fact is,' he began coldly, trying not to sound as angry as he felt, 'my stepson is merely escorting the young lady to the circus.'

And changing to a safer topic: 'The show was excellent, the clowns were particularly fine. Where do you go next?'

'Down to the Borders, then across to Galloway. Willie of course was just here for the one night, especially for the Queen. What a nerve to make up a poem for her like that. Didn't you think so?'

'I thought he did very well. It was very brave of him.'

'I suppose so.'

Faro was relieved to end the conversation as someone called Briggs' name.

Turning on his heel Briggs suddenly swung round to face Faro again. 'They never found why my lassie drowned, those Dundee police.'

'So I understand.'

'I will never rest until I find out why she did it. And if there was a man involved, I'll kill him.' Briggs studied Faro intently as if trying to read his thoughts. 'The police say the case is closed.'

Guiltily, Faro remembered Ramsey's post-mortem, and how the doctor had certain knowledge that Polly had been murdered but was powerless to do anything about it. He hated lying to Briggs but there were too many innocent people involved and he had given his word to Vince.

'I expect they did their best,' he said lamely.

'I doubt that their best is good enough. And it doesn't bring my lassie back. Pity you hadn't been on the case, Inspector. I hear that you always get your man.'

'Well, not always, Briggs. Just sometimes,' he added sadly.

There was no more to be said and with a brief salute Briggs went back to the circus tent.

Faro watched him for a moment, noting the weary defeat of his shoulders. Briggs looked stooped and old and Faro felt suddenly ashamed that he had been angry with him. Angry with himself, too, and wishing that he had been asked by the Dundee police to help find Polly's murderer, who was probably still at large.

As was the murderer of Rachel Deane. There was not the least doubt in his mind about that.

Vince was at breakfast next morning, reading *The Scotsman*, when Faro put in an appearance. He had slept badly.

'That was a splendid party afterwards, Stepfather.

Pity you missed it, you should have been there. All this chasing of criminals is very well, but not when it seriously interferes with a chap's social life.'

And pointing to the newspaper: 'Willie got a mention here for his performance. He'll be pleased about that.'

Faro said nothing, pouring himself a cup of tea. He didn't feel particularly hungry.

Vince smiled across at him. 'What, no breakfast? Anyone would think you had had a high old time, wining and dining last night. Is there something you aren't telling me about? A secret assignation?'

Faro grimaced. Obviously Vince was back again in his old teasing manner. He should be grateful for that.

Vince had returned to his newspaper. 'Good Lord. Good Lord. Sir Arnold is dead. Here it is. Late notice. Died in the early hours of this morning.' He looked across at Faro. 'He's been very poor ever – ever since—' He still found difficulty in alluding to Rachel's death. 'A bit wandered, poor old man.'

He sighed. 'Wilf will be in full charge now. I don't suppose it'll make any difference to me, but I'm sorry. I shall miss Sir Arnold. He's been good to me.'

Faro dreaded that Sir Arnold's funeral, coming so soon after Rachel's, would reopen that well of sadness for Vince, only now healing.

Chapter Seventeen

Vince returned two weeks later, full of information about Sir Arnold's funeral, one of the largest Dundee had ever seen.

'Brought it all back to me, so soon after Rachel. The graveside, the vault. All that sort of thing,' he said sadly.

As usual he spent the entire weekend with Kathleen. After the first rather uncomfortable evening, Faro had not renewed his invitation for her to dine with them at Sheridan Place, although he realised guiltily that he must do so soon.

However, it was a very subdued Vince who returned from taking Kathleen out to dinner on the Sunday evening.

'I will be taking the 6.25 train tomorrow morning, Stepfather,' he said, looking in to say goodnight. And opening his bedroom door: 'By the way, I might not be home again for a little while.'

At Faro's questioning look, he said: 'I made up my mind tonight to ask Kathleen to marry me.'

'And—?'

'She declined my proposal.'

Faro felt a curious sense of relief as Vince continued:

'Everything seemed so right and it would have made the McGonagalls very happy—'

'You don't marry someone to make their relatives happy, dammit,' Faro said sharply.

'I know that. But I am rather disappointed.'

159

Disappointed he might be, thought Faro shrewdly, but hardly heartbroken. There was nothing here to resemble his grief at losing Rachel.

'Did she give any reason?' Faro asked.

'The best. She has a lover already. That explains so many things, doesn't it? Seems to have been going on for quite some time. In fact, he set her up in the milliner's shop.'

Here then were Faro's own suspicions of the rich protector confirmed, first by Briggs and now by Kathleen's own admission, which he felt considering the ardour of Vince's courtship was somewhat overdue.

Mistaking his stepfather's expression, Vince said: 'It isn't as immoral as it sounds.'

'I didn't say it was. You should know by now, lad, that I'm quite unshockable.'

Vince nodded. 'She says he loves her and in her own words, once his present circumstances leave him free to propose, and he gets his life sorted out, they intend to marry.'

'Is there a wife already?'

'Sounds like it, although she was very reserved about discussing his affairs. Said she had promised him never to tell anyone and she was only telling me because she knew she could rely on my discretion.'

His glance invited affirmation and when Faro was silent, he went on: 'Apparently he's quite high up – her words – and it would be disastrous for his position in society if all this was made public. At least it explains her "touch me not" attitude. She confessed that she was very attached to me and that in normal circumstances, she would have been honoured to be my wife, etc., etc.'

Pausing he added bleakly, 'Or so she said last night.'

Faro put a hand on his arm. 'I'm sorry, lad. You seemed quite smitten.'

'Not to mind, Stepfather. There are more fish in the sea, as you once reminded me,' was the pseudo-cheerful reply. 'Actually we didn't have a lot in common, you

160

know, I see that now. Not enough for a lifetime, at any rate.'

And as an afterthought: 'Perhaps the real reason I was attracted to her in the first place was that I was looking for another Rachel. And she did remind me of her, at first sight. But that wore off after the first meeting.'

And observing his stepfather's anxious look, he smiled. 'Not to worry, I'll be all right this time, I promise. Who knows, two rejections, maybe it'll be third time lucky.'

'I hope so, lad.'

Vince was silent, studying the doorknob gravely. 'Oh by the way, talking of proposals and so forth, I have another bit of news that will surprise you. Now that Wilf has inherited, his engagement to Lady Clara Wilkes will be announced shortly.'

He smiled. 'He told me very confidentially as we drove down together, but I'm sure he won't mind you knowing, since you are the soul of discretion. Lady Clara is an heiress of ancient family whose estates are in Fife.'

'This is all very sudden.'

'Oh yes, totally unexpected, Stepfather. She's a remote cousin. Her husband ran off with another woman, an Italian princess, I understand. Wilf and she were childhood sweethearts and have been secretly engaged for some while, with Sir Arnold's blessing. Now that her divorce has come through they are to marry quietly, without any fuss, since the Deanes are officially in mourning.'

'A very well-kept secret.'

'Oh indeed. And it explains what I could never understand. Why someone as eligible as Wilfred hadn't married long ago. Even for dynastic purposes.'

But Wilfred Deane's newfound happiness was not destined to last.

* * *

161

Two days after the announcement in *The Scotsman* Faro was summoned to the Royal British Hotel where a man had been found dead in his room.

On Princes Street the church bells were summoning worshippers to morning service, while inside the hotel Sergeant McQuinn was waiting for him and a uniformed constable kept curious hotel guests and alarmed staff at bay in the corridor.

Inside Room 102, the police surgeon Dr Holmes knelt beside the corpse who lay wide-eyed and staring as he had fallen.

'Haven't touched a thing, Inspector. I've just arrived, waiting for you to make your inspection of the room.' He pointed to the body where a tiny red rose of death had bloomed and congealed on the immaculate white shirt-front.

Faro looked around. It was an almost tidy scene of death, no visible bloodstains, only a chair overturned and a broken ornament near the door. The bedcovers had apparently been dragged off in some sort of struggle but the bed itself had not been slept in, for its pristine pillows were undented.

As Holmes began to examine the body, Faro leaned over.

'Anyone found the murder weapon? A knife with a stiletto blade, I would say, since there is so little blood about.'

'Correct, Inspector. Stabbed once, a bull's-eye straight to the heart. Died instantly.'

McQuinn and the constable had followed Faro inside and were methodically searching the room. An easy task since the drawers and wardrobe were empty, the dead man's travelling bag unpacked.

'No evidence of the knife so far, sir. Guess the murderer carried it away with him.'

'How long has he been dead?' Faro asked the police surgeon.

'Oh, by the condition of the body, I would say at least

162

twelve hours. Between ten and midnight last night.'

McQuinn handed Faro a piece of paper. 'According to reception, the deceased is one of their regulars. He had no visitors last night. His wife usually comes with him, but he was alone this time. Just as well for her, perhaps.'

And looking over Faro's shoulder: 'He's a Mr James Burnett, a businessman from Arbroath. That should be easy to check, sir. At least we have an identity for him.'

Faro looked at the body. 'I think you'll find that Mr Burnett isn't his real name.'

McQuinn whistled. 'So it's not going to be a simple case after all.'

Faro smiled wryly. 'After all your years with me, McQuinn, I shouldn't have to tell you that murder is never simple.'

'Any ideas, Inspector?' asked the police surgeon as he drew a sheet over the body.

'Yes. I know this man. His name is Wilfred Deane.'

'Of the Dundee Deanes?'

'The same.'

'Good Lord. This will cause a sensation.'

'Didn't I read that he was about to be married?' said McQuinn. 'Then I wonder—'

'I think you'll find that the lady calling herself Mrs Burnett was not Lady Clara Wilkes,' said Faro, examining the room.

Apart from the bedcovers on the floor, the lack of a struggle suggested that Deane had been easily over-powered and that death had come to him as a surprise.

'That stiletto stabbing suggests an Italian job to me,' said Sergeant McQuinn. 'There's a lot of them about in Edinburgh these days. Could be a vendetta. Fallen foul of one of their families.'

When word reached Superintendent McIntosh, he was mortified that an illustrious and prominent Dundee citizen should have been murdered in his territory.

'Dundee Police are sending a detective. He's already

on his way but you will be in charge of this case, Faro.'
A pause. 'Any ideas?'

'Any ideas?' asked Detective Sergeant Elliott. He arrived
that evening at Sheridan Place off the same train as Vince
who came in his official capacity as Deane's doctor, horrified to hear of his friend and employer's brutal murder.

Both men exchanged grumbles about the atrocious rail
journey. Both were in agreement about one thing. 'High
time they got that bridge finished.'

'This wasn't a murder for theft,' said Faro in answer
to Elliott's question. 'Nothing of value was taken. His
pocket case was full of bank notes, his watch and rings
intact.'

'Bad business,' said Elliott. 'Any suspects?'

'Just one. Woman calling herself Mrs Burnett, his only
regular visitor. As they knew her well, she did not bother
to register. But the bellboy met a heavily veiled woman
making her way to Deane's room on Saturday evening.
When he said: "Good evening, Mrs Burnett," she ignored
him. He thought perhaps he had been mistaken.'

'Or she was anxious not to be recognised,' said Elliott
slowly.

'Did anyone see her arrive or depart?' Vince asked.

'No one,' replied Faro.

Elliott looked crestfallen as only a detective can when
deprived of evidence to link the main suspect with the
murder.

'Any other ideas, sir? I understand you both knew
the victim.'

'We had a slight acquaintance,' said Faro.

'Good, that is a great help. For motive, and so on.'

'I think I can assess from the state of the room how
the murder was accomplished and from the evidence, this
case has all the marks of the crime passionel.'

'A woman's crime, is that it, Stepfather?'

'Do I take it you have hopes of an early arrest,
Inspector?' Elliott interrupted. And seizing upon Faro's

non-committal response as affirmation: 'Excellent. Well, well, I never expected this kind of progress. You are certainly living up to your reputation, sir.'

Faro smiled wryly. 'First catch your murderer, Elliott.'

'I would say it's an open and shut case.'

'Yes indeed,' said Vince enthusiastically. 'Ten to one it is the missing Mrs Burnett.'

'The hotel staff were very eager for a bit of gossip. Apparently Mr and Mrs Burnett were never seen in the dining room like any other married couple, honeymooners apart. Had all their meals in the upstairs suite,' said McQuinn. He had been very busy, very thorough with his interviews at the hotel.

'And being wise after the event, the manager said he thought it highly suspicious that a gentleman allegedly from Arbroath should choose the weekend to conduct his Edinburgh business and receive visits from his wife.'

'I expect Sergeant Elliott knows that Mr Deane had recently become engaged,' said Vince.

'Indeed yes. The Wilkes are very well thought of, a highly respectable family. There is going to be one hell of a scandal when we have to investigate Lady Clara's alibi. Ever met her, Dr Laurie?'

'Not yet.' Vince looked at his stepfather. 'I suppose it is just possible—'

Faro shook his head and said to the detective, 'You're wasting your time. I think you will find that the lady is completely innocent and can account for her movements that night. Also it will come as a considerable shock to her to learn that Deane had a mistress in Edinburgh.'

'A shock to everyone who knew him, Stepfather.'

'And neither lady with any inkling of the other's existence,' said Elliott thoughtfully. 'So if Lady Clara is innocent, all we have to do is find this other woman.'

'That could be quite a poser,' said Vince. 'But I'm sure my stepfather is up to it.' He smiled. 'He is probably one jump ahead of us right now.'

'We need only go as far back as Deane's engagement.

I fancy that came as a startling surprise to Mrs Burnett. And fortunately I know exactly where I can lay hands on the lady who calls herself by that name. If you would care to accompany me.'

He turned and looked at his stepson who was listening eagerly.

'You too, Vince lad.'

Vince laughed uneasily. 'Why me?'

'Because you know the way better than I do.'

'You don't mean— Oh no, Stepfather. You can't—'

'I do. And I'm afraid I must.'

Chapter Eighteen

It was a very silent quartet who were deposited by the police carriage in Rose Street. First, Detective Sergeant Elliott and Sergeant McQuinn, to take notes in case an arrest was made, then Vince, shocked into stunned silence by the information that he was to step inside the shop and behave in a casual fashion.

Last to emerge was Faro, clutching a parcel whose contents he did not see fit to divulge. 'Best wait outside, lads.'

'We don't want to alarm her,' said Elliott firmly. 'We don't want any unnecessary violence. But we had best be prepared, Inspector,' he added, patting his greatcoat pocket significantly. 'Let's try to act as normally as possible, Dr Laurie.'

It was doubtful, thought Faro, whether anyone could regard that white stricken face as normal, and he gave his stepson a rallying pat on the shoulder.

As Vince walked to the counter, Faro hovered by the door while Elliott and McQuinn looked through the window keeping the scene under careful scrutiny while trying to remain inconspicuous. It wasn't easy, two tall men and a uniformed constable, who was the driver, all gazing with elaborate concentration at a windowful of ladies' bonnets.

They saw the pretty young assistant step forward, shake her head.

'Come along, Elliott,' said Faro and threw open the door.

As they spread themselves before her, the assistant eyed them with alarm.

'No, I'm afraid Madame is not at home to anyone.'

'I am a friend of hers,' said Vince.

The girl considered his companions doubtfully. 'Madame is indisposed.'

'She will see me,' said Vince winningly and striding purposefully behind the counter opened the door leading upstairs to the flat.

'You can't do that,' protested the girl. 'Wait – I'll lose my job for this.'

Elliott and McQuinn pushed past her up the stairs. Faro paused before a tray of milliner's accessories then he followed them.

They found Kathleen slumped in a chair by the window. There was something in her attitude which touched an unhappy memory for Faro. She looked up at them with a wan smile.

'I've been expecting this visit, gentlemen.' She turned her gaze to Faro, said softly, 'You've come to arrest me, haven't you, Inspector?' And nodding vigorously, 'Yes, I did it. I killed Wilfred Deane.'

Faro heard a sigh of relief from Elliott. There was going to be no violence, just a confession and a peaceful arrest.

'I'm glad you've come,' she said, rising wearily, supported by her hands on the arms of the chair. 'Strange, it's better to be taken by friends.' Looking intently at Vince, 'By people who care about what happens to you rather than by impersonal constables who are merely doing their duty.'

'Have you the murder weapon, Kathleen?' asked Faro. 'You used a long hatpin, like this one,' he added, flourishing that same article used by ladies to stab their hats into submission, which he had picked up from the counter downstairs. 'Am I right?'

Kathleen's face paled, her hands flew to her throat as if she felt the rope around it. For a moment he thought she was about to faint.

'Will they hang me?' she whispered.

'Sit down, lass,' he said not unkindly. 'We'll do the best we can for you. It was self-defence, after all, was it not? May I?' And leaning forward he pulled aside the silk scarf she wore. On her neck, on either side of her throat, were two ugly bruises.

Vince swore. 'Did he do that to you?'

Before she could reply Faro said, 'Be so good as to pour a glass of water for her, will you please.' And to Elliott, 'You see I was perfectly sure that when Miss Neil visited the hotel room that evening as Mrs Burnett, she had not the least intention of murdering her lover. He had summoned her as usual, but this time with the express motive of getting rid of her.'

'Surely that's a bit steep,' said Elliott. 'I mean, if he was just breaking it off—'

'Bear with me, if you please. Deane had excellent reason for not "just breaking it off" as you call it. He had to shut Miss Neil's mouth for good. Believe me, gentlemen, his whole future was at stake. And if anyone had murder in his heart that evening, it was Wilfred Deane. And when he attacked her, so brutally and unexpectedly, she used the first and only weapon to hand – the long pin which had secured her bonnet.'

He paused and looked down at Kathleen. 'Perhaps you would like to tell us in your own words what happened, lass.'

As Kathleen spoke, she threw occasional glances of appeal and apology in Vince's direction. 'When I first met Vince I told him—'

'If you please, lass, we'd like to hear it right from the beginning. How and where you first met Wilfred Deane. This will all need to come out in court,' Faro added to McQuinn who had taken out his notebook in readiness.

'I met Wilfred Deane when I was working with Uncle Willie McGonagall in the factory. He isn't my uncle really,' she said, 'just a remote cousin who was very kind after my mother died. Anyway, he got me a job in the jute factory, hoping to train me for the stage. He wanted me to be a Shakespearean actress. But I was never any good at that.

'One day when Wilfred was visiting the factory he came and talked to me. I felt very flattered. He came often after that and I guessed that he was taken with me. Of course I played up to him, he was a wealthy man.'

She paused. 'To cut a long story short, after we became – intimate – he bought me this shop in Edinburgh. He didn't want anyone to know and I was to pretend that I had gone to London. I didn't mind, I would have done anything for him. Anything.'

The word was a whisper, her sigh remembered. 'He asked very little in return. Just that he might come and visit me when he was able to do so. He often has business meetings to attend here. I agreed. Who wouldn't? After life in the factory, it was a very good exchange. And after my early life in a Dublin slum,' she added bitterly.

'When Sir Arnold died and Wilfred inherited I presumed the family opposition to his marrying me that he talked about would be at an end. No one could disinherit him now for marrying a former factory girl. The whole of Deane's was his now. I had a note – I have it here somewhere – to meet him as usual for the weekend at the Royal British Hotel.'

From her reticule she produced a crumpled piece of paper which she handed to Faro. 'But this time I was in for a shock. I wasn't prepared to find out that everything he had told me and had promised was a lie. He told me to prepare myself for bad news. He could not marry me, first of all. He had to marry this Lady Clara, but this was to be a marriage of convenience. He needed Lady Clara's money to keep Deane's afloat, but he did not love her.

'I was to rest assured that I was his one true love and there was no reason why we should not continue as before, this arrangement had worked so well. Of course

I was very upset and disappointed. I wept. I had waited all this time for him to be free to marry me. I had no wish to remain in the backwater of his life as his mistress, seeing him only when he could visit Edinburgh.

'We never went outside the hotel in case we were recognised. I was always heavily veiled. What kind of life was that? I wanted to be at his side – as his wife, living at Deane Hall. I wanted children too,' she added bleakly.

'When I told him all this, he kissed me, assured me that I was worrying unnecessarily. Do you know, he never once lost his temper. So patient with me, smiling, understanding.'

Taking a deep breath, she continued painfully. 'As he held me, he removed my bonnet, loosened my hair. As he usually did before – before—'

Her sudden pause, eyes wide, relived that moment. In panic she was suddenly aware of this audience of men.

'We quite understand, lass,' said Faro hastily.

She shook her head tearfully. '"Never worry, my dearest. We will think of something. Rest assured of that." And those were his very last words to me. He shook down my hair, let it fall about my shoulders, put his hands round my throat. I thought he was about to caress me. I closed my eyes.'

Her voice faded and her hands trembled towards the bruises. 'But his grip grew tighter and I saw in his eyes reflected in the dressing-table mirror that he meant to kill me. The room was growing darker. I struggled frantically. I'm quite strong really and I pushed him hard, he let me go. But as I tried to reach the door he came at me again, knocked me down with his fist.

'I fell beside the bed, put out my hand to struggle to my knees and felt my bonnet – with the pin still sticking out of it. He turned me to face him, his hands tight around my throat again and I struck at his chest with all my might.

'You know the rest,' she ended wearily and, sobbing, buried her face in her hands.

171

As Faro went forward, put a hand on her shoulder, she looked up. 'I've sat here for the past two days, trying to summon up courage to give myself up. The waiting was worse than seeing you coming up the stairs, I can tell you. I'm glad you came. Now I can be peaceful. Will they hang me, Mr Faro?' she asked again.

'I think when all your story is known, no jury will convict you, Kathleen. There would be a public outcry against any such verdict. Especially as you saved the hangman a job.'

'I don't know about that, Faro,' said Sergeant Elliott.

'Let me finish,' said Faro. 'A public outcry, since Wilfred Deane is himself a murderer—'

'Hold on, Faro. Attempted only—' Elliott protested.

Faro shook his head. 'Deane has already committed murder and escaped justice. As Kathleen well knows.'

It was Kathleen's turn to protest. 'I don't know anything about that, sir. Honest I don't.' But there was panic in her voice, terror in her eyes.

'I think you do. You see, I believe all your story. Except for the first part. You weren't being quite straight with us, were you? About Deane's reasons for not marrying you? Oh, it is true he was going to have to make a marriage for business reasons with a woman whom he did not love. But you knew about that right from the beginning. He made no secret of it.'

'I never did. I never did,' she cried. 'I swear I didn't know of Lady Clara's existence until I read it in the newspapers.'

'Ah, but it was not Lady Clara he told you he was being forced to marry when he confessed his predicament to you originally. It was nearer home. Much nearer.'

Kathleen bit her lips and turned away sullenly as Faro looked across at Vince. 'It was Rachel Deane, as we both know. He told us so that night she died. How much he loved her.'

'He never loved her,' Kathleen shouted. 'That was a rotten lie.'

'It was indeed,' said Faro, 'for love didn't enter into his cruel calculations. It was money again. Money he desperately needed to save himself from jail.

'Time was running out. He knew there was already a fraud and embezzlement enquiry under way regarding the inferior building materials that had been substituted for the more expensive ones contracted for the Tay Bridge.'

Elliott nodded. 'So you knew about that too, Faro?'

'Superintendent Johnston told me in confidence.'

'These enquiries are the main reason why this damned bridge is taking so long in the building. It was no secret with us. We all knew about that on the force. Go on, Inspector.'

'Wilfred Deane was desperate to lay his hands on Rachel's fortune. He might have succeeded but she fell in love with someone else, someone she had just met briefly. Her grandfather's doctor, namely Vince here. And that was when he decided to murder her.'

'But that can't be true, Rachel took her own life. We saw her,' said Vince. 'Good God, Stepfather, you were there.'

Faro shook his head. 'Would you do something for me, Kathleen?'

When she looked doubtful, he said: 'It might well strengthen your case, save your life.'

'All right,' she agreed sullenly.

'Would you please remove your shoes.'

'My shoes? If that's what you want.' As she kicked them aside, Faro withdrew from the bag he carried a pair of ladies' slippers.

At his side, Vince's cry of painful recognition was added to Kathleen's gasp of alarm.

'Those were Rachel's,' said Vince. 'She wore them that night – and you've kept them all this time,' he added accusingly.

'I know, lad, I know. And I've kept them with good reason, for just such an occasion as this. Kathleen, if you please.' Kneeling down he took her feet and slipped on first the right slipper and then the left.

And looking up triumphantly, 'As I suspected. They fit perfectly. Made for this lass. Gentlemen, I've waited for months to find this particular Cinderella.'

'Are you mad, Stepfather? That's a mere coincidence. Those were Rachel's shoes,' Vince protested.

'Then why didn't they fit her? You tried them yourself when she was recovered from the river. They kept falling off. The reason, although we were both too distressed to note its significance at the time, was that they were several sizes too large for her.

'Why? Because they were Kathleen's shoes and it was Kathleen who ran away from you that night and climbed the ladder on the bridge.'

'But how – how—'

'Hear me out. It was Kathleen who climbed the ladder. But it was Rachel who plunged or was thrown to her death in the River Tay.'

Chapter Nineteen

Vince stared open-mouthed at Faro. 'What are you saying, Stepfather. We saw Rachel jump—'

'No, we didn't. It was not Rachel. And she did not drown. She was probably already dead—'

'But we were there when they took her from the river.'

'Oh yes, two hours later. Time enough for her to give all the appearance of having drowned. A post-mortem, however, might have revealed that she was heavily drugged.'

Vince continued to shake his head in bewilderment, gazing at his stepfather as if he had taken leave of his senses.

Faro put a hand on his arm. 'Vince, lad, I know this is going to be terrible for you. But believe me, Rachel was probably already dead when her body plunged into the Tay. Drugged, carried up the iron pier by Deane in one of those huge baskets the workmen used for transporting materials from one level to another—'

'But the letter I received,' Vince interrupted, having found his voice at last. 'That was from her. I knew her writing. I had other notes, dammit.'

'Oh yes, indeed. She wrote the letter. I haven't the least doubt about that. She had been kept prisoner in the house since she returned from Errol. Carefully watched from the moment she announced to Deane that she was going to marry Dr Laurie. And what was more her grandfather would have been delighted when she told him.'

Ignoring Vince's groan of anguish, Faro continued:

'Deane was desperate, so he shut her up in her room, explaining to everyone that she was suffering from one of her periodic bouts of madness. Vince, lad, Rachel was never mad. Wilful, difficult but more spoilt than anything by being a rich man's only granddaughter. But mad, no. The madness was dreamed up by Wilfred Deane. That was his invention.

'He realised he couldn't keep her prisoner for ever. Time was running out for him. Rachel would inherit on her birthday. Meanwhile the police were investigating a possible fraud. And if he could not replace the vast sums of money he had been systematically embezzling from the firm, then he would be disgraced and go to jail.

'He had to have Rachel's money to set the accounts right. He couldn't drag her to the altar unwillingly or without her grandfather's permission, especially as the doting old man was prepared to accept her choice, namely the young doctor he had taken such a liking to.

'There was only one way out. And so he decided to kill her, make it look like suicide. He didn't anticipate much difficulty in then getting the money from Sir Arnold on the grounds that a sick old man was incapable of handling the firm's finances. Everyone was sympathetic and the shareholders had known for some time now that Deane's was being run by Wilfred.

'Perhaps he had been considering getting rid of Rachel also for some while. Certainly from that first moment he saw Kathleen in the factory and noticed that there was a resemblance.'

Pausing he looked directly at Kathleen. 'Was that when he began to formulate what must have seemed like a clever but extraordinarily foolproof plan, using you as an innocent accessory?'

When she turned away, he went on: 'But to return to that fatal evening on the bridge. He went to Rachel, said he had had a change of heart. He had decided to let her marry you after all, Vince. But she must go that night, elope, before anyone could stop her.

176

'How eagerly then she must have written that note to you. Dear Wilfred was being so helpful, he even brought her one of the maid's dresses and a cheap shawl, a uniform garment which could easily be obtained for Kathleen too.'

Looking at his stepson's white face, he said: 'I'm sorry, lad. This is very distressing for you. Because the moment Rachel wrote that note she had unknowingly signed her own death-warrant.

'Deane then administered the drug, most likely in a cup of tea to fortify her for the journey, or by some other seemingly innocent means. Then he took her out in his carriage until the drugs took effect. He knew about Dr Ramsey's discoveries concerning Polly Briggs and so Rachel had to be kept alive to make it look like drowning for the Procurator Fiscal's report.

'On the bridge the workmen had gone and it was already dark. He had bribed the night-watchman to look the other way while he carried in Rachel's body and deposited it in the basket. The watchman little realised that Deane would make sure he never lived to enjoy that substantial bribe, though I doubt if even he – unless he was a very good actor indeed – knew the contents of the basket he was helping his master to elevate by the pulleys up to the top platform.

'Deane then climbed the ladder himself and began his vigil. There was one more assignation to keep before his plan could succeed.

'And this is where you came in, Kathleen. What was it? How did he persuade you? Just one more impersonation.'

'One more? What do you mean – one more? I swear—'

Faro held up his hand. 'I mean this was the second time you had pretended to be Rachel Deane. The first was at Deane Hall when she denied ever having met Vince.'

When she didn't reply, he said: 'I am right, am I not? Come along, Kathleen,' he added sharply. 'It's all gone too far to go back now. And you won't help anyone, least of all yourself, by concealing the truth.'

Kathleen stared at him mutinously as if about to refuse. Then suddenly defeated, she said: 'All right, I'll tell you what happened. But I swear to God I'm innocent of Rachel Deane's death. I knew nothing of what he intended when I agreed to appear as Rachel Deane that first time for Vince's benefit. Only that he had made a wager with one of his friends.'

She smiled. 'Wilfred loved gambling, he couldn't resist it. That was how he got heavily into debt. I didn't think his request was strange, because he often wagered on daft things. This one was that he could pass me off as Rachel Deane, to fool this friend who would be hiding behind the screen with him. It was, he said, all a bit of a lark but if he won the wager, a thousand guineas, then I should have as my reward my milliner's shop – this place.'

'Paid for, as you now realise, by Rachel Deane's death,' said Faro grimly. 'Have I been right so far?'

She shrugged. 'Yes, and I wish to God you hadn't. I would do anything to undo what happened that night.'

'Pray continue.'

'I never guessed that the reason he was first taken with me was that with dark hair instead of fair, he thought I could be made to look like Rachel. Then at a Saturday night social he heard my 'Song of the Forest', realised that as a born mimic I could probably imitate a human voice as easily as bird calls.'

She sighed. 'I loved him right from the start. He convinced me that this impersonation was all a harmless joke to trick his friend, but I would have done anything for him, anyway. Whatever he asked without question.'

'Did you ever meet this friend?'

'No. I doubt now whether he ever existed. Just another lie,' she added with a bright bitter smile.

'Did you ever go to London?'

'No, that was for Uncle Willie's benefit, so that they wouldn't worry. I was to stay in Deane Hall. Of course in order to impersonate Rachel I had to spend some time with her. There was no difficulty.'

'Did you never meet anyone?'

'Sometimes I saw a maid in the distance who looked the other way – or dived into the linen cupboard, the way the gentry treat their servants.'

'How was your presence explained to Rachel?'

'Oh, that was easy. I was a dressmaker and milliner and very good at making wigs too. I ran a very exclusive establishment and only visited clients in their own house. I could be recommended. Rachel welcomed me. She was a trusting gentle creature, pretty and a bit vain.

'She liked the idea of having a wig made too. It was quite usual in her station in life. She was as much a fool as I was. I stayed several days to give her fittings and by that time I could do an exact imitation of her voice. It wasn't too difficult after bird calls – the human voice, I mean.

'Wilfred was very pleased. Although in a strong light I couldn't have fooled anyone, in a dimly lit room, with Rachel's voice, he said the result was quite uncanny.'

'And as long as you didn't stand up,' added Faro, 'since you are two inches taller but more slightly built. Your face might pass muster but not the rest of you. And your feet and hands are larger too.'

Pursing his lips, he studied her for a moment. 'That was another thing that bothered me. Why, in all that heat of passionate denouncement when you said you had never met Vince before in your life, you never once got up from that huge armchair, not even to ring the bell.'

'I thought the difference in our shape would be noticeable.'

'And of course, you couldn't hope to make these appearances too often.'

'Wilfred had said only once at Deane Hall. Later he told me that it had been a dress rehearsal. The friend was making a fuss about a thousand guineas and was unwilling to pay it. He thought I had done very little. So

there was to be one more appearance. The friend wanted
something more daring before he would pay up.

'He wanted to see Rachel Deane on the bridge in
moonlight. I was scared at first, but Wilfred said it was
quite safe and so I agreed. I would meet him on the
bridge, wearing a bonnet to conceal my hair. He also
insisted I wear a plain dress, like a maid's. And a plain
bonnet. I couldn't think – and he wouldn't tell me – why
he wanted two exactly the same.'

'Because it was essential for his plan that you and
Rachel were dressed alike. And of course you couldn't
wear a wig this time. It might have fallen off. Then all
would indeed have been revealed. When you attacked
Vince, you entered the yard by the broken fence—'

'Wilfred had arranged that, I knew exactly where
to look for it.'

'So you ran to the bridge, kicked off your shoes to
make the climb easier. Tell me, why did you carry a
stone in your reticule?'

Kathleen looked uncomfortable.

'Was that to deter Vince should he succeed in following
you?'

'I think that was what Wilfred intended,' she whispered,
her eyes downcast.

At Vince's horrified gasp she turned to face him.
'Don't look so shocked,' she said viciously. 'I never
loved you. It was always him I wanted. I would have
done anything for him. Anything. You meant nothing
to me.' She snapped her fingers. 'Not even that much.
Nothing at all.'

She began to weep noiselessly as Faro continued:
'May I tell you what happened next? When you climbed
to the second platform behind the pier, you ducked back.
Wilfred came forward and heaved Rachel's body from
the bridge.'

'I swear I didn't know that was what he was going to
do. I was sick with fear. He told me later that she had
to die or go into the bedlam. She was quite insane and

he was doing her a kindness. I swear I would never have agreed, if I'd known it was just her money he was after. And that everything he had told me was a pack of lies.'

There was a pause and Faro said, 'After it was done, you both waited until we ran down to the river. Then you both put on workmen's overalls and while all attention was diverted to the search for Rachel's body, you came back down the ladder. Two workmen who had been inspecting the scene of the accident.

'Wilfred then discarded his overalls and reappeared as if he had just arrived. As a matter of interest, what did you do?'

'I went to the station and took the morning train to Edinburgh.' Kathleen wrung her hands. 'I was horrified by what had happened. You have to believe me, I never had any idea until that night that he intended to murder Rachel.'

'Although you knew he had murdered before. When he got rid of Polly Briggs.'

Her face flushed guiltily. 'I don't know anything about that.'

'You might as well admit it, Kathleen. It will all come out in court. But this time you were not involved. Although you must have had your suspicions.'

'Oh all right then. Polly Briggs was jealous when she saw that Wilfred liked me. She was determined to get even so she struck up with a fellow high up in the office. Charlie something-or-other.'

'Charlie McGowan?'

'Yes, him. She told me he wanted to marry her but he had a wife already. And the wife had found out and was going to leave him. Then she told me an extraordinary story that Charlie was hoping to go into partnership with Deane's. He was very clever at his job, but he had also found out something that would give him a hold over Wilfred Deane.'

'And you told him?'

Again she coloured. 'Of course I did. I thought it

was only proper to warn him. I didn't want him to go to prison. I would have done anything to save him from that.'

'How did you feel when you heard that Charlie McGowan was dead?' Faro asked coldly.

'That was an accident, Wilfred told me.'

'And you believed him. What about Polly?'

'I thought she had committed suicide, because of Charlie. Perhaps she was in the family way.'

She saw by Faro's expression that he didn't believe that either. 'You're very clever, Inspector. But how did you guess all this?'

'I assure you I did not guess. Those are not my methods at all,' said Faro sternly. 'I observed and deduced and came to what I am far from happy to realise was the right one. The only conclusion I could make in the sorry mess you have made of your life.'

With a grim smile, he added: 'But you very nearly got away with it. I was completely baffled. Oh, I had clues all right but nothing that fitted or made sense. You have your Uncle Willie to thank that you were found out.'

'Uncle Willie? How on earth did he know?'

'He didn't. But if we hadn't been invited to his performance at Holyrood the other evening—'

'I don't see what—'

'Of course you don't. But when I saw the magician's trick with the girl who apparently dived into the flaming tank and then saw her resurrected, unscathed, back on the trapeze, I realised that two girls were involved. That was the piece that had been missing all along from my calculation. Once it was in place, I knew exactly how Rachel's death had been stage-managed.'

As they watched her led away, she turned to Faro a last time:

'Will Uncle Willie and Aunty Jean be involved?' she asked anxiously. 'They have been so good to me. Like parents. I wouldn't want them to be hurt.'

'I'll do my best.'

182

Afterwards Vince said to him. 'Do you know, Step-father, I think she was lying. That she knew he intended to kill Rachel but was prepared to look the other way. Her story is fairly thin in parts.'

'I dare say we will have it all in detail before the trial is out.'

'There must be some good in her. I mean, she was worried about the McGonagalls, about a scandal for them.'

Faro suppressed a smile. 'Scandals never hurt an actor, lad, they thrive on it. Sensational news will simply add lustre to his notoriety. And notoriety is something always to be welcomed. Only being totally ignored can damage an actor like William McGonagall.'

Epilogue

The Deanes are fictitious but the tragic consequences to be paid for dubious dealings concerning the Tay Bridge is a true story.

Sunday 28 December 1879 dawned unseasonably mild but with an unnatural stillness which amateur astronomers put down to the brief eclipse of the moon due just before sunset. At 4 p.m. it began to rain heavily and retired admirals and sea-captains who resided in handsome villas on both sides of the Tay disgustedly laid telescopes aside.

Barometers were consulted and the sudden fall noted while in leafy avenues and parks, gardens were crushed as if a giant foot had stepped upon them and great trees bent under the weight of the rain.

By 5 p.m. the east wind had increased to gale force. As the first roof slates and chimneys crashed to the ground those about to depart for evening service had second thoughts. Rattling windows and sounds of broken glass as conservatories were demolished recalled uneasy memories of the gale twenty years earlier. It had flattened entire forests and whisked out of the earth ancient trees of enormous proportions.

In Edinburgh although the weather had worsened considerably the 4.15 'Edinburgh Express' left Waverley Station on time, reaching Granton twenty minutes later. After a particularly ferocious voyage across the Firth of Forth the passengers reached Burntisland where Engine 224 prepared to leave at 5.20. Relatively new, built in 1871, it pulled four five-compartment carriages. One first class, one second and three third. Last of all came the luggage van.

The description of 'The Edinburgh' as an express was optimistic since it stopped at every station. However the increasing gale did not slow down its leisurely progress across Fife.

Meanwhile Dundee's Tay Bridge Station was in the full grip of the storm. There was consternation as the wind roaring through the tunnel had burst out with a violent explosion, carrying away part of the handsome glass roof and leaving a trail of destruction. A similar tale was being reported from Dundee's main streets, littered with plate-glass windows blown out of shops, while the normal Sabbath quiet of the suburbs was shattered by a crescendo of flying chimney pots, tiles and uprooted trees.

At 5.50 the local Newport train crossed the Tay Bridge. Carriages rocked alarmingly from side to side and seemed to lean over in the full blast of the storm. The sparks which flew from the wheels convinced the terrified passengers that the train was on fire. The guard assured them that this sparking effect was quite common in such weather, caused by the wind pushing carriages so that the flanges of the wheels ground against the guard rail.

With sighs of relief from passengers and railwaymen alike the train safely reached the shelter of the now shattered Tay Bridge Station. The happy ending of one story was the prelude to tragedy, for the passing of the 5.50 had pushed the bridge to the very limits of its endurance.

In the words of one observer there was 'a continuous roar punctuated at intervals by ferocious blasts' as the gale hurled itself upon the bridge. It tore and relaxed its grip momentarily, tore and relaxed again, a gruesome tug o'war over the iron girders and the battered, beseiged columns.

At 7.13 the 5.20 from Burntisland rushed towards the bridge. The gale pounced upon it, roaring like some

185

savage animal devouring its helpless prey. The train see-sawed dangerously, trembling and the high girders hung by a thread.

In Tay Bridge Station, a few intending passengers and railwaymen paced the platform impatiently. The Edinburgh Express had been signalled as it entered the bridge. It was now 7.23 and something was amiss. The telegraph was dead. The signalbox was over the Esplanade and a signalman rushed to meet them. Yes, there were still signal lights on the south end of the bridge where the train had entered. Perhaps it had stopped for some unknown reason but the telegraph lines were down.

They ran back towards the station where two men said they had seen fire falling from the bridge at about 7.15. Another had seen great spumes of water rising from the river at about the same time. Two railwaymen set off to walk the bridge.

At 9 p.m. the training ship Mars, which had been anchored near the bridge approached. A wave of expectation, a whisper of 'survivors' rippled through the now large crowd.

A few bewildered crewmen came ashore. The deck watch had seen the train on the bridge, had observed its lights entering the high girders. His attention distracted momentarily by the storm, when he looked again, the moving lights strung out in a line had vanished and there was apparently a long break in the bridge's outline.

The Newport ferry arrived. It had been grounded since 6 p.m. by low tide. Here was the first link with the south shore and the possibility of survivors but because of the storm and difficult currents, the ferry had been unable to get anywhere near the bridge.

Mailbags had been washed up at Broughty Ferry, plus reports of debris along the shore all the way from Ladybank to Monifieth.

Provost Brownlie shook his head. 'I'm afraid the bridge is down then; no doubt about it. And the train's gone too.'

Dundee newspapers were already setting up tomorrow's headlines: 'Terrific Hurricane – Appalling Catastrophe – Tay Bridge Down – Passenger Train Hurled into River – supposed loss of 200 lives – '

'The scene at Tay Bridge Station tonight is simply appalling. Many thousands of persons are congregated around the building, and strong men and women are wringing their hands in despair . . . '

As newspaper reports go, this was a restrained piece of journalism.

On Monday 29 December the sun rose at 8.47 a.m. Slowly the bridge began to take shape, a giant monster unbending from sleep and a great sigh arose from watchers lining the shore from Broughty Ferry to Magdalen Green. All night long, praying that rumour lied, they had awaited this moment and the irrefutable evidence of their own eyes.

Now the cruel morning light revealed the central piers, 'like columns of some majestic ruin of antiquity', all that remained of the high girders.

The Queen had sent a message. 'Inexpressibly shocked we feel most deeply for the two hundred passengers and all those who have lost friends and relatives in this terrible accident.'

The agent who had checked tickets at the last station before the bridge arrived. He clutched fifty-seven tickets, told of two seasons tickets and perhaps a dozen more passengers travelling past Dundee, seventy-five dead was substituted for the estimated number who travelled regularly by that same train on weekdays.

The news flashed across the nation by electric telegraph and swamped headlines on the Afghan war and the storming of Sherpur. It brought to readers everywhere a chilly sense of national betrayal and disbelief that Imperial Britain who ruled the waves and half the civilised world – with pretensions towards the other half – and could build anything better than any other nation, had been caught out.

187

The desks of harassed editors were littered with indignant letters: how could Britain be let down in the eyes of the world by a bridge that dared to fall? Other letters from cranks believed it was God's judgement on people who used wheeled transport on the Sabbath.

And so Hogmanay, the greatest day of celebration and inebriation in the Scottish calendar became just Wednesday 31 December, on which divers discovered the train. It had plummeted down with the girders, like a bird trapped in a cage. The engine's throttle was still open, the brakes unapplied, proof positive that the train had just entered the high girders when they fell. Any bodies would have been washed away towards the sand flats and five pounds reward was offered by the Council for every body recovered. Search parties patrolled night and day, their torches eerily pricking the darkness with pinpoints of light while whalers, superstitious to a man, shook their heads. Seven days must pass after a drowning before the river god would release his victims for Christian burial, on the eighth day.

The body of one victim, Ann Cruickshank was recovered. A maid from Kilmaron, unimportant and obscure in life, at her funeral with every honour, Dundee buried all seventy-five of the Tay Bridge disaster victims.

A Court of Inquiry decided that the bridge had been badly designed, badly constructed with shoddy materials and maintained with shoddy workmanship. Twenty men had died in its building and seventy-five men, women and children in its fall. The first contractor died before his contract could be taken up, the second went insane and died.

The disaster fund had raised two thousand pounds, with a generous £250 from Sir Thomas Bouch. His bridge with its unlucky thirteen girders had got him a knighthood and brought death and disaster to Dundee. Elected scapegoat, it was with some satisfaction that the citizens learned the design of the Forth Bridge in Edinburgh was to be taken away from him, pending enquiries and all work upon it was to cease.

Bouch survived only four months after the report destroyed him. His melancholia advanced into madness and when he died on 1 November the Tay Bridge disaster had claimed its last victim.

One of the chief characters however had a surprising resurrection. Engine 4-4-0 No 224 was not permitted to end her days a rusting wreck, a constant memento of Dundee's greatest tragedy. She was gathered together, repaired, refitted and put back into service, where she remained for another forty-five years. Not without reason, she was known as 'The Diver'.

The high girders too were lifted from the river bed. Sold as scrap to a company of locomotive engineers in England and made into railway engines, each bore a small plate recording the origin of its metal. Many continued into the twentieth century.

The last word must go to William McGonagall, for Inspector Faro was right in his predictions. Long forgotten as a tragedian, dubbed by posterity 'Scotland's Worst Poet', he is remembered for his 'Beautiful Railway Bridge of the Silvery Tay'.

Good Heavens! The Tay Bridge is blown dcwn,
And a passenger train from Edinburgh,
Which filled all the people's hearts with sorrow,
And made them to turn pale
Because none of the passengers was saved to tell
  the tale
How the disaster happened on the last Sabbath
  day of 1879
Which will be remembered for a very long time.

It must have been an awful sight
To witness in the dusky moonlight,
While the Storm Fiend did laugh, and angry did
  bray
Along the Railway Bridge of the Silvery Tay,
I must now conclude my lay

By telling the world fearlessly, without the least
    dismay,
That your central girders would not have given
    way,
At least many sensible men do say,
Had they been supported on each side with
    buttresses,
At least many sensible men confesses,
For the stronger we our houses do build,
The less chance we have of being killed.